On Calm Water

Susan Harding

The Conrad Press

On Calm Water
Published by The Conrad Press in the United Kingdom 2024
Tel: +44(0)1227 472 874
www.theconradpress.com
info@theconradpress.com
ISBN 978-1-916966-94-9
Copyright ©Susan Harding 2025
All rights reserved.
Typesetting and Cover Design by: Levellers
The Conrad Press logo was designed by Maria Priestley.
Printed and bound in Great Britain by Clays Ltd, Elcograf S.p.A.

Introduction

This book is about a young girl who experienced sexual abuse at the hands of her Father when she was just five years old. The memories made her feel scared and tearful. However, when she found love and faith in Jesus, all her fears vanished, and she found peace like calm waters. The gentle love of Jesus gave her the strength to move forward. She found new strength in following Jesus and felt overwhelming love and peace. The love she received from her Heavenly Father was utterly different from that of her earthly Father, who had caused so much turmoil. His actions had a long-lasting impact on her childhood, pushing her into a stormy experience.

The written account reflects the personal perspective of a young girl as she navigates through a harrowing experience, portraying her emotions, inner turmoil, and eventual resilience. The vivid descriptions of her fear and vulnerability during the storm, along with her longing for comfort and security, provide a deeply personal insight into her psychological journey. The story aims to convey the young girl's inner world, her courageous struggle for survival, and her unwavering hope for solace in the face of overwhelming despair. Through the detailed portrayal of her thoughts and emotions, the story invites readers to empathize with her and gain a profound understanding of the impact of her traumatic experiences. Overall, the story offers a poignant and intimate portrayal of the young girl's perspective as she grapples with adversity and seeks healing and peace.

Chapter 1 On Calm Water

The tranquillity of the water was so overwhelming. The sea surface was smooth as glass reflecting the sunlight. Turquoise waves sparkled under the bright sky like a cascade of sparkling diamonds. The wave's soft murmur was like a lullaby that lulled her to sleep. Miniature waves lapped lazily against her boat. A golden glow spread across the sky. A massive expanse of crystal-clear water was all that she could see. The sun was such a beautiful colour, which seemed to be a mix of orange and pink that filled the dark blue sky and gave colour to the fluffy white clouds. The calm seas reflected these fantastic colours in a way they only could, and the effect of the colours made the scene like one in a painting. It was so peaceful. She closed her eyes and felt the warmth on her face. Then suddenly, she opened her eyes and heard a thunderstorm in the distance. The waves were dull, mirroring the overcast sky; bursts of light burnt across the crest of the oncoming storm, and the darkness was engulfing any spec of light. She closed her eyes just as another lightning flash bolted from the sky. She felt a cold shiver all over her body. She was all by herself caught in this storm.

As the little girl huddled in the boat during the ferocious storm, her mind was a whirlwind of emotions. She felt a profound sense of Fear and vulnerability, heightened by the relentless crashing of the waves and the overwhelming darkness of the ocean. In that moment, she longed for her Mother's comforting embrace and guidance, yet her unanswered pleas deepened her feelings of isolation. The boat where the young girl takes refuge during the storm is a small, weather-beaten vessel, its wooden planks worn smooth from years at sea. The scent of salt and aged wood permeates the air, mingling with the sharp tang of seawater. The boat rocks and creaks with each onslaught of the waves, its rhythmic and unsettling movements, as if it carries the weight of the girl's tumultuous emotions.

The boat's interior was a patchwork of peeling paint and frayed ropes, with remnants of past repairs visible in mismatched wood and faded stains. A single oar rests against the side, its metal tip worn to a dull gleam from use. The girl clings to the rough fibres of the boat's edge, finding a precarious sense of security in its familiarity as the storm rages around her.

As lightning illuminates the sky, the boat's interior is briefly revealed in stark relief, casting elongated shadows that dance across its confines. The girl's fingers trace the grooves and imperfections of the wood, seeking solace in the tactile reassurance of the boat's presence amidst the storm's chaos. The howling wind and rain drumming against the boat become a dissonant symphony, underscoring her isolation and vulnerability.

Despite its weathered appearance, the boat serves as her sanctum in the tempest's heart, a fragile but resolute haven that mirrors her inner resilience. Each lurch and roll of the vessel mirrors the tumult of her emotions as she seeks refuge within its confines, grappling with the churning turmoil within and without.

The storm became a powerful metaphor for the turmoil she had experienced in her young life. Each crash of the waves mirrored the chaos and fear she felt inside, while the vast expanse of the lonely ocean intensified her helplessness. The little girl's internal struggle was between her tenacious hope for survival and the despair threatening to engulf her.

Her Fear manifested as a tightening knot in her stomach, and every lightning flash and thunderclap felt like a physical manifestation of the emotional turbulence within her. Her unmet longing for security and comfort from her Mother only amplified her fierce emotions, leaving her adrift in a sea of uncertainty and Fear.

As the little girl huddled in the boat during the ferocious storm, her actions reflected her inner turmoil. She sought refuge in a corner of the boat, wrapping her arms tightly around her knees as a protective instinct kicked in. Her eyes darted anxiously, alternating between watching the crashing waves and scanning the dark, overcast sky for any sign of respite.

With each lightning flash, she flinched and instinctively pulled herself closer into a ball, seeking shelter within herself. The thunderclaps seemed to reverberate through her very being, intensifying the sense of vulnerability and Fear that gripped her. Despite the tumultuous surroundings, she maintained a semblance of control, engaging the boat's sides to steady herself as it rocked violently on the agitated waters.

Amidst the chaos, she silently whispered prayers, her lips moving in a passionate plea for safety and deliverance. Each wave that crashed against the boat sent a shiver through her, yet she clung onto a fragile thread of hope, refusing to succumb to the overwhelming despair that threatened to engulf her. It was a poignant depiction of a child grappling with the forces of nature and her inner turmoil, seeking solace and security amid a relentless storm.

The little girl's thoughts and emotions during the storm reflected the deep-seated impact of her traumatic experiences. Despite the overwhelming turmoil, her resilience and hope for survival shone through, offering a glimpse of inner strength that would eventually guide her towards healing and peace.

The storm unleashed its fury, casting an eerie glow over the darkened sky as the lightning cracked through the atmosphere and the distant rumble of thunder echoed ominously. The little girl called out to her Mother, using the endearing term "Mummy." However, she sensed an air of distance and frailty about her Mother, who did not offer any response. The little girl yearned for her Mother's comforting embrace and guidance, but when her pleas went unanswered, she was engulfed by a profound sense of isolation and vulnerability. Her emotional journey was marked by turbulent waves of Fear and an intense yearning for security, and her Mother's absence served only to amplify these fierce emotions.

This is her journey that would test her resilience and faith.

Years later, this child, now a woman of 68, finally experienced the calmness of the water. The gentle breeze gave her the strength to carry on. She found a new strength in her faith, following Christ, and the love and peace that overwhelmed her. She felt the love from her Heavenly Father, someone she could trust in, not like her Earthly Father, who, in her Perception, caused the storm that surrounded her. His actions, which she interpreted as overpowering, affected her, continuously pushing her further into the storm. The memories of his intimidating presence and actions haunted her, instilling Fear and insecurity. The description of him shaking and throwing her around painted a picture of a frightening and abusive figure whose actions left a lasting impact on her. However, she found solace and strength in her faith, ultimately finding the love and peace she longed for in her Heavenly Father.

When memories resurfaced as a five-year-old, she often felt overwhelmed with emotions and shed tears. These tears concealed deep-rooted fears that haunted her. However, she discovered solace and comfort when she developed a deep connection and love for Jesus. This love helped her conquer her fears and find inner peace.

The storm was unrelenting, with waves crashing against the rocks and the boat swaying violently. Lightning flashed, and thunder roared, creating an atmosphere of chaos and turmoil. Overwhelming darkness and loneliness enveloped her as she fought against the brutal waves. The howling wind and the icy water added to the sense of danger and despair. It was a harrowing experience, fraught with Fear and uncertainty. She fought with all her might, clinging to the hope of survival amid the storm's turmoil.

The calmness of the water was a stark contrast to the storm's chaos. She felt a sense of tranquillity as the waves settled, and the once turbulent sea became still. The gentle breeze gave her strength and peace, and she found solace in the newfound calmness. The stillness of the water offered a moment of respite from the relentless battering of the storm, and the serene atmosphere provided a much-needed sense of relief and reassurance.

Despite her Father's imposing figure, Fear, and shaking, she held on.
This is a testament to her unwavering resilience, a quality that would guide her through the storm and inspire those who hear her story with hope and inspiration.

The sky blackened, and she was engulfed in darkness. She felt herself sinking deeper into the frightening abyss. A profound sense of loneliness and insecurity consumed her. A tall, hefty figure kicked her continuously until her bruised body could take no more. This child had fearful eyes and glimpsed another figure in the darkness. This figure was frail. She suddenly recognised this person as her Mummy, but she tried calling her to help her, but there was no response. Her emotional journey was tumultuous, filled with Fear and a deep longing for safety.

She lay there shaking with panic. The darkness was still upon her, but there was no movement. She heard only the waves lashing against the side of the boat. She dared not move, and it seemed like hours that she lay there. The waves peaked alongside her, and she could look into their jade-green depths. Surrounded by the veil of darkness, she keenly perceived her elder sibling's familiar, reassuring presence by her side. Amid the darkness, she could feel the comforting presence of her elder sibling, offering her a sense of support and safety during this difficult time. The young girl's older sister played a crucial role in her life during those harrowing times. Despite being subjected to the same abuse, her sister became her source of solace and strength. They shared a unique bond born out of mutual understanding and the burden of their traumatic experiences. In moments of distress, the older sister offered unwavering support, providing a comforting presence that brought a glimmer of reassurance amidst the darkness they both faced.

Their shared struggles created an unspoken closeness, and the young girl often found refuge in her sister's protective embrace. During the most challenging moments, they sought comfort in each other's company, holding onto a fragile sense of sisterly solidarity that helped them navigate the turbulent waters of their childhood. The siblings' unspoken empathy and silent exchanges spoke volumes, offering a lifeline of understanding and compassion amid their shared ordeal.

Despite facing the same stormy seas, their bond became a source of resilience and fortitude, a silent promise that they would weather the storm together. In each other's presence, they found a fleeting reprieve from the turmoil, holding onto moments of shared joy and closeness amidst the overwhelming challenges they confronted. The older sister's unwavering presence and silent understanding became a beacon of hope, reminding the young girl that she was not alone in her journey towards healing and restoration. Her older sister, who was also a victim of their father's abuse, struggled with her own emotional and psychological trauma. This made it difficult for her to always be by her younger sister's side during the abuse. As both girls coped with the aftermath of their experiences in different ways, the older sister found it challenging to provide constant support while dealing with her own pain and healing process. Despite her genuine love for her younger sister, she grappled with internal battles, sometimes hindering her ability to protect and comfort her sibling. Their journeys to overcome the abuse and find healing are depicted as complex and intertwined, reflecting the profound impact of their shared trauma. The little girl felt alone despite her older sister also going through abuse. Each person's experience of abuse is highly individual, as trauma can deeply affect emotions and reactions in profoundly unique ways. While her sister was going through a similar situation, the little girl's internal struggles, fears, and feelings of isolation were deeply personal to her. Trauma can impact individuals differently, and the little girl's sense of loneliness might have been influenced by a variety of complex factors related to her emotional journey. It's essential to recognize that even within the same family or shared experiences, each person's response to trauma can vary significantly. The knowledge that her older sister was enduring similar abuse while being unable to see her during the storms of abuse intensified the young girl's feelings of heartache and despair. Despite understanding the shared trauma they both faced, the young girl grappled with a profound sense of powerlessness and aching sorrow at not being able to provide comfort and support for her sister. The awareness of her sister's suffering amidst her struggles deepened the young girl's feelings of helplessness and anguish, amplifying the emotional weight she carried. She longed to offer solace and protection to her sister, yet the inability to do so fueled her inner turmoil and desperation. The absence of her sister's visible presence during those harrowing moments of abuse compounded the young girl's yearning for connection and solidarity, adding a layer of poignant complexity to her own experiences. The little girl and her older sister supported each other through the abuse they had experienced, even when the little girl felt lonely and her sister wasn't physically present during the abuse. In moments of solitude and distress, the little girl held onto the memories of her sister's comforting presence and the shared understanding they had developed. While physically apart, the emotional support they provided each other was a source of strength. The older sister's unwavering love and understanding resonated with the little girl, offering a sense of solace and reassurance during her most difficult moments. Despite the physical separation, the profound bond between the two sisters became a beacon of hope and resilience, helping them navigate the lingering effects of the abuse they had endured.

Her tired hands clung desperately to the side of the boat as she longed for respite from the biting wind and the relentless gale that had suddenly surrounded her. Her only solace was the hope that the wind would soon subside, allowing her to find peace in the tranquil waters. The calmness of the water was like a soothing balm for her weary soul. The sea's surface was a picture of tranquillity, with gentle ripples creating mesmerising patterns that seemed to dance in the sunlight. The serene waves lapped against the boat, creating a rhythmic and comforting melody. The water, clear as glass, reflected the azure sky above, creating a sense of vast serenity that enveloped her. The stillness of the water offered a moment of respite, a temporary escape from the tumultuous journey she had endured. The gentle lapping of the waves and the peaceful expanse of the sea provided a much-needed sense of relief, evoking a profound feeling of calm and tranquillity.

She saw a flicker of light. A wafer of the moon broke through and laid a wriggling silver track on the waves. The moonlight cast a shimmering silver trail on the tranquil waves, creating a captivating and serene scene. The moon's soft glow danced on the water's surface, adding a touch of ethereal beauty to the surroundings. The gentle ripples of the water reflected the moon's radiant presence, evoking a sense of calm and tranquillity amid the nighttime serenity. But the wind still hammered. The boat still rolled through the toppling seas. This small child was slowly drifting into the coldness of the night, and she could not survive.

Then, someone came out of the darkness as though from nowhere.

She reached out her hand, and he took it, squeezed it tightly, and spoke, "We're both going to be alright."

When he touched her hand, she leaned over the side of the boat. "It looks so peaceful", she said. She felt a flood of relief at his appearance, a reassurance that she was not alone. A volume of air in the freshening wind filled her eyes with tears. It had been a harsh night, but someone she didn't even recognise had taken a moment to acknowledge her feelings, to share her loneliness. Those precious words he had spoken were to remain with her on that long and exhausting journey and touch her naturally.

JESUS CALMS THE STORM - MARK 4 V 37-39
And a great windstorm arose and the waves beat into the boat, so that it was already filling . But he was in the stern, asleep on a pillow. And they awoke him and said to Him. "Teacher do you not care we are perishing"? Then he arose and rebuked the wind, and said to the sea, "Peace be still" And the wind ceased and there was a great calm.

Chapter 2: The Raging Storm

As the small boat ventured deeper into the churning waters, a massive wave rose from the horizon, its imposing presence casting a foreboding shadow over the turbulent seas.

Suddenly, a huge wave crashed over her, engulfing the boat. She fought for control against the raging water, and another wave pushed the boat along. The boat being rocked backwards and forwards by the relentless waves was an instinctive and disorienting experience. As the little girl huddled in the boat during the ferocious storm, the sound of crashing waves echoed like thunder in her ears, intensifying her sense of isolation. The salty scent of the sea mingled with the damp, musty odour of the wooden boat, creating an atmosphere of raw, elemental power. Every lightning flash illuminated the world in stark, blinding white while the subsequent darkness enveloped her in an oppressive shroud. The relentless rocking of the boat sent shivers through her body, and the cold droplets of rain felt like icy fingertips tracing patterns on her skin. In this moment of chaos, she clung to the frail hope that faith and love had instilled in her, whispering prayers carried away by the tumultuous wind. Each motion seemed to amplify the turbulent storm raging around her. As the boat pitched and rolled, she struggled to maintain her line of calmness on the water.

She maintained her balance, feeling the full force of the elements against the fragile vessel. The rhythmic back-and-forth movement created a sensation of being at the mercy of the mighty sea, evoking a mix of Fear and awe at the relentless nature of the storm.

"I'm sinking," she cried as the boat tilted sideways and backwards. Cold water began to pour into the boat, and she had only minutes before it would be submerged. As her eyes adjusted again to the darkness, she noticed someone rising out of the water. She was determined to survive, to battle against those brutal waves. She leaned over to grab him tightly, her determination shining through the darkness.

The lightning sliced the darkness, and she tightly fastened her arms around his neck. She tried several times. He slipped from her grasp for just a minute. The swirling water inched closer to her. She fought to hold her footing. Her feet and fingers were so numb with the cold as she clung on for dear life, and then suddenly, a strong gust of wind swept across the waters, and the wind thundered past her and slammed against the side of the boat. She lost her footing, and a colossal swell tipped her into the water. The feeling as she was tossed into the water was one of utter disorientation and terror. The shock of the cold water enveloping her felt like a sudden plunge into a world of chaos and uncertainty. Each wave seemed to snatch her breath away, and the relentless churning of the water disoriented her senses. Her body instinctively thrashed against the weight of the waves, her limbs feeling heavy and unresponsive amidst the tumult. In that harrowing moment, she clutched onto the remnants of faith and love, desperately seeking a lifeline to guide her back to the surface. The icy water slapped at her face. Sharp stabbing pains struck her side; once again, she found herself confronted by the imposing, towering figure. The pain continued. I'm drowning she shouted, and then she heard this quiet voice in her ear.

""I am in control," he declared firmly as he grabbed her and carefully guided her back into the boat. Confused, she uttered, "How did I end up here?" The little girl felt relief and gratitude when rescued from the water. As she was pulled onto the rescue boat, she clung to the rescuer, feeling a mix of emotions overwhelming her. The sense of being saved from the terrifying storm and the treacherous waters brought tears of joy and lingering fear to her eyes. She found solace in the reassuring presence of the rescuer and felt a glimmer of hope for the future. Safe in the arms of this person who had come to her aid, she knew she was no longer alone in facing the challenges that life had thrown her way. As the storm raged amidst the chaos and turmoil, her mind was a whirlpool of emotions, memories, and fears that threatened to consume her. She traversed the tumultuous seas of her past, each wave of memory crashing against the shores of her consciousness. The overwhelming darkness enveloped her, echoing the feelings of loneliness and insecurity that had plagued her for so long. Yet, amid the relentless battering of the storm, a glimmer of hope emerged as she clung to the newfound strength and love she had discovered in her faith. She understood that her older sister was also facing abuse, but she always felt her sister's support by her side. At times, despite her absence, though, she experienced profound feelings of solitude. Even though she was engulfed in her own turmoil, the young girl couldn't shake the constant worry and heartache she felt for her older sister, who was also enduring abuse. It added another layer of anguish to her already overwhelming emotions. She grappled with a profound sense of helplessness, unable to provide the comfort and protection her sister desperately needed. The weight of their shared suffering weighed heavily on her heart, intensifying her feelings of fear and vulnerability. Despite her own struggles, her concern for her sister remained a constant source of anguish, deepening the complexity of her emotional turmoil.

During the harrowing ordeal, her mind turned to her earthly Father, whose overpowering presence had been a source of turmoil and Fear. The memories of his menacing figure loomed large, intertwining with the crashing waves and the howling winds. Despite the overwhelming anxiety and pain, she found solace in the love and peace she discovered in her relationship with Christ, a stark contrast to the tumultuous dynamics of her past. Even though she had found comfort in Jesus, her older sister was still struggling to cope with the trauma of their shared experiences. Despite her sister's initial attempts to create a sense of routine and protect her younger sibling, the weight of their past continued to burden her. She grappled with feelings of guilt and helplessness, often withdrawing into a shell of emotional distress. While the younger girl found solace and strength in her faith, her older sister battled internal turmoil, struggling to find her path to healing and peace. The stark contrast in their responses to the trauma highlighted the complexity of their individual journeys and the unique ways in which they sought to overcome their shared pain.

As she grappled with the treacherous waters, she struggled to reconcile the trauma of her past with the glimmer of hope that she now held onto so fiercely. It was a battle of resilience and survival, a testament to the strength she had discovered within herself. The waves of Fear and loneliness threatened to engulf her, but she clung to her faith as the lighthouse that guided her through the storm. In the depths of her despair, she reached out for a lifeline, a beacon of hope in the darkness, ultimately finding comfort in the reassurance that she was not alone.

Throughout the stormy journey, she grappled with the haunting memories of her past, each wave of trauma colliding with the fragile vessel of her resilience. As she battled the relentless storm, she sought to navigate the disruption of her emotions, her mind a whirlwind of Fear, determination, and, ultimately, a newfound sense of strength and faith. The weight of her past bore down on her, yet in the depths of the storm, she found the courage to confront her pain and emerge with a glimmer of hope and resilience.? Am I alive?" She gulped for air.

The storm's intensity heightened as the dark clouds surged across the sky, blotting out the sun and casting an ominous shadow over the vast expanse of the ocean. As the girl huddled in the small boat, the sea surged and roared, sending chilling tendrils of mist and spray that stung her skin. The smell of salt and dampness filled the air, mixing with the metallic tang of Fear that seemed to linger on her tongue. The boat pitched and rolled with each crashing wave, the relentless assault of the water causing her stomach to churn and her heart to race.

The howling wind whipped through her hair and clothes, carrying an icy bite that seemed to seep into her very bones. Rain pelted down like a furious onslaught, splattering against her skin and drenching her to the core. Each droplet felt like a sharp sting, and the relentless drumming on the boat's surface added to the cacophony of the storm.

Amidst the chaos, the girl's grip on the boat's sides tightened, her knuckles turning white as she struggled to maintain her precarious hold. The boat creaked and groaned under the strain, lurching with every tumultuous swell. The deafening crash of the waves reverberated through her, vibrating within her chest and leaving her breathless.

Amid the tempest, the girl's thoughts were consumed by a whirlwind of emotions, her mind echoing with the pounding of the waves. She felt as if she were a speck adrift in a whirlpool of uncertainty, the relentless assault of the storm reflecting the tumult she felt within.

The child tossed about like a rag doll and felt the raw power of the sea as she clung desperately to the side of the boat. When the storm finally subsided, she peered over the edge and beheld the serene stillness of the water, a sharp contrast to the chaos that had just gripped her. The air was heavy with the scent of salt and moisture, and the gentle lap of the waves against the boat provided a soothing rhythm to the newfound tranquillity. Yet, as the lightning flashed and the thunder echoed in the distance, she knew the respite would be short-lived. She was petrified. The person who rescued her from the water sat beside her in the boat.

She looked into his eyes, "Who are you?" I want my Mummy.

It was calm again, but for how long? She was hurt and confused and lay there huddled in the corner of the boat, shaking and terrified with Fear and coldness. She felt the chilliness of the night creep around her yet again. She slowly opened her eyes and saw the same reassuring, kind face looking down upon her. He whispered into her ear, "I love you," then she closed her tired red eyes and drifted off to sleep.

Chapter 3: Seeking Light

Amidst the darkness that had consumed her, she yearned for a glimmer of hope to illuminate her path.

She suddenly awoke in great fright and lost all Perception of time. "This is a nightmare; I have to wake up," she said. Her anxious eyes turned skywards at a scattering of black clouds. She saw strange looming shapes and wondered which shapes meant good and which meant harm. Someone made a sudden appearance, then disappeared without a trace. She felt highly helpless and sensed the strong presence of violence in her memory, leaving a lasting impact.

"There was a shimmer of light, and she saw a figure, which she watched intently. She opened her mouth, but no words came out. She tried to remember everything that had happened the night before, but the memories were too painful to confront.

The mist in the sky hid the bright full moon. She could hear distant voices, and her heart was pounding. She stared into the darkness, trying to pinpoint the source of the sound, but she could not see anything. That night, she hardly slept and gazed in amazement for several minutes at the waves rippling over the water's surface. Gradually, after a while, she felt herself drifting towards sleep again.

The morning arrived swiftly, appearing serene at first. The tranquil blue water flawlessly reflected the sky in a way it never had before. The little girl felt a deep calmness as she gazed upon the still water. Its smooth surface seemed to exude tranquillity, and the gentle ripples that occasionally danced across it only added to the peaceful atmosphere. The calmness of the water enveloped her, creating a soothing and serene environment that allowed her to feel content and at ease. As she watched the water, all her worries seemed to melt away, leaving her with a profound sense of tranquillity and inner peace. She instantly noticed some movement and caught the echo of a voice.

She gazed intently across the water and discerned a silhouette. The figure called out to her, "Trust in me." At first, she was filled with Fear, but his gentle encouragement compelled her to move towards him cautiously. She was undeniably resilient. It would have been so effortless to surrender, but her determination refused to waver. Gripping the boat's edge with all her might, she suppressed the pain, resolute in her decision to hold on tightly. "I believe my Mother will find me. This person will inform her of my whereabouts, and she will come to my rescue." With sudden resolve, she released her hold on the boat and reached out to him. He swiftly lifted her out of the boat, and for the very first time, she experienced a profound sense of safety and warmth from within.

In a tender embrace, she clung to him, gazing deeply into his eyes, her face awash with tears. He gently ran his fingers through her hair, wiped the moisture from her eyes, and comforted her with his soothing presence. "Please don't go," she pleaded, "Just let me hold your hand a little while longer." As he withdrew his hand, she was left alone once more. At first, tears cascaded down her cheeks quietly, but soon, her sorrow erupted in powerful, heart-wrenching sobs.

For an hour or so after he had left her, she felt very hot and then cold and shivery. Waves of panic started to shoot up her spine. A voice called out her name. She froze with terror. She hid behind a nearby rock. The figure approached her; His eyes burned at her. It was her Father. He lowered himself upon her; he caught her at her side with his big, sturdy boot. A careless move from her would cause him to bring down his fists with great force. She tried to escape, but he was too firm. "Help me!" she cried. He vanished. She felt humiliated and prayed for help. Then, she felt a rush of love and heard someone reaching out to her. He reached out his arms and bent down to her. She looked slowly around and saw the beautiful countryside beneath the expanse of the sky filled with drifting clouds. She felt safe. The peacefulness of the countryside provided her with a much-needed escape. The serene atmosphere, the tranquil surroundings, and the countryside's natural beauty calmed her mind and lifted her spirits. The gentle rustling of the leaves and the soothing sounds of wildlife surrounded by lush greenery with tall trees lining the path on both sides. She could hear the soft rustle of leaves in the gentle breeze as the trail wound through the picturesque countryside. The sunlight filtered through the branches, creating dappled patterns on the forest floor. The air was filled with the earthy scent of moss and the distant sound of birdsong. It was a serene and peaceful setting. The sweeping landscapes offered her a sense of tranquillity and solace. It was where she could find respite, gather her thoughts, and reconnect with herself. She struggled to stand but eventually got on her feet despite feeling bruised. The person with her had disappeared, and she was walking along a winding road.

Night fell quickly, and she could hear music in the distance while casting shadows under the moon moved across the trees. In the distance, she saw a church steeple and the sound of music was coming from that direction. Although her incredible courage to survive and carry on, the difficult time she was going through was quite overwhelming. But how much longer could she hold on? A wave of tenderness for her strength and courage swept over her, and she prayed again that she would soon see her mummy. Her legs felt weak, like jelly, after walking for an eternity. The distant church appeared miles away, and the journey had become disorienting and challenging. She was at a crossroads as the temperature dropped, and her feet ached with blisters. Despite the hardships, she made the brave decision to push forward. Although stumbling along the way, she chose to rest for a moment, gathering her strength to continue her courageous journey. She observed the sunset and was struck by its peacefulness, stunning light, and warmth. Without realising it, she briefly fell into a deep slumber.

In her dreams, the church appeared as a refuge and solace. Its towering spire reached towards the sky like an outstretched hand, offering guidance and reassurance. As she stepped inside, shafts of sunlight filtered through the stained-glass windows, casting colourful patterns on the stone floor. The air was filled with a hushed reverence, and she felt embraced by a sense of peace and belonging. The church's pews seemed to stretch endlessly, inviting her to sit comfortably in the quiet sanctuary. The sound of a distant choir filled the air, wrapping her in a warm, comforting embrace. As she walked through the dream church, she was drawn to the altar, where a soft glow seemed to emanate, symbolising hope and faith. Each corner of the church carried a sense of serenity and acceptance, providing a haven for her troubled spirit.

The sudden realisation hit her that it had all been a dream, and she awoke.

As the darkness swallowed her whole, she felt herself plummeting into the unknown. Uncertain of her surroundings, companions, or even the day, she waited anxiously for her racing heartbeat to slow down gradually.

She wandered through the woods, surrounded by the calming sound of flowing water. Suddenly, a faint rustle in the woods caught her attention, making her alert and curious. She observed footprints surrounding her and subsequently perceived the sound of gravel. A silhouette advanced toward her in the darkness, prompting her instinctual response to close her eyes. "Can this situation endure further?" Slowly reopening her eyes, she uttered a cry of distress, "Please go. I am unable to endure this any longer." Then, she abruptly recognised the figure as her Mother and desperately clung to her. Her tear-streaked face was swollen and red. Holding onto her was a young girl with dark, grieving eyes. "Mummy, you have found me," the girl said softly. She attempted to confide some details about her unsettling encounters with her Father, hoping to observe her Mummy's reaction. She felt a twinge of Fear that her Mother would react with anger. Instead, her Mother responded with deep silence and withdrawal. Her Mother unexpectedly laughed nervously as she gathered her thoughts to speak again. This was different from the reaction she had anticipated. The child's face turned ashen as a look of Fear overcame her. Her muscles tensed up, and a sudden surge of electrical impulses raced through her brain like a wildfire, causing a flash of light to flicker behind her eyes.

She lost sense of what was happening to her. Her words became muddled, and she slowed down mentally and physically. Weak-kneed and shaking, she stumbled and must have lost consciousness for a while because when she awoke, she was very disoriented.

Her Mother was warm, compassionate, and strong-willed, always putting her family's needs first and radiating love and care. The little girl's feelings toward her Mother were a mix of adoration, dependency, and a longing for affection. When her mum nervously laughed, the little girl's feelings toward her Mummy were a combination of confusion, uncertainty, and a hint of concern. The little girl's Mummy appeared frail and seemingly unresponsive when the girl called out to her in her time of need. The little girl longed for her Mummy's help and support but felt lonely and insecure when she received no response. The emotional journey of the little girl was tumultuous, filled with Fear and a deep longing for safety, and her Mummy's absence intensified these feelings. Her heart pounded heavily in her chest, a wild rhythm that mirrored her escalating panic. She desperately scanned her surroundings, hoping to find anything to grasp onto, but her frantic movements only yielded emptiness. Overwhelmed by a wave of crippling guilt, she fought to contain the rush of emotions threatening to consume her. The dark, expansive void she was plummeting into seemed to stretch infinitely before her, and she could sense herself being inexorably drawn into its depths. A disorienting panorama of the distant water below loomed as she descended, intensifying the vertigo and deepening her despair. Amidst the chaos, a voice urgently called out her name, persistently tugging at her, refusing to let her slip away. Despite her valiant efforts, she made a frustrating little headway in her struggle to climb back up. I can't imagine how terrifying and disorienting it must have been for the little girl as she fell into the black hole. The profound loneliness and insecurity she experienced at that moment was heartbreaking. It must have been incredibly frightening for her, especially with the darkness engulfing her and the feeling of sinking deeper into the abyss. The imagery of a tall, hefty figure kicking her repeatedly and the frail figure of her Mother being unresponsive only adds to the haunting nature of the experience. It's a testament to her strength and resilience that she could endure such a harrowing ordeal. All she could comprehend was that her survival depended entirely on her resilience. With her strength waning and a feeling of utter helplessness, sweat trickled down her face as the water below loomed closer. Suddenly, she looked up and spotted a familiar face signalling to her. She extended her hand to grasp the lifeline and smiled through her tears.

In the oppressive darkness, the little girl managed to extricate herself from the deep, confining hole with every ounce of strength she could muster. As she emerged, she trembled like a fledgling falling from its nest.

This person yet again reached down and lifted her out, pulling her from the water below and enveloping her in a sense of safety and tranquillity once more. He held her close, enveloping her in his arms as he caressed her hair tenderly. Tears of joy streamed down her face, gleaming in the soft light. Overwhelmed by exhaustion, they sought solace in each other's embrace, allowing their tears to flow as they held each other tightly.

Amidst her deep pain, she found solace in a small yet powerful display of compassion. The person reached out to her, offering heartfelt words of comfort and instilling hope for better days. Their connection had grown strong, and her countenance would visibly brighten in his presence.

She now truly believed that this person was indeed Jesus, and he would guide and protect her through her long journey.

Chapter 4: Embracing the Unknown

The nights seemed to stretch endlessly, and despite her best efforts, she couldn't shake off the feelings of guilt and Fear. The Fear of being abandoned by her Mother haunted her despite her belief that Jesus was watching over her.

Each night became more terrifying than the last, as she lived in constant dread of her Father hurting her once again. She sat for a while; she had survived.

For some time, safety was present, yet sobs escaped her as she grappled with her emotions. The presence of her Father's aggression seemed ever-present. She instantly felt his proximity again as he moved towards her, but she endeavoured to fend off his actions. His eyes travelled gently across her face, a warm smile lighting up his features. In return, she offered a fleeting yet slightly hesitant smile. She felt a growing sense of unease as his intense gaze bore into her. As he drew nearer, she could feel his eyes tracking her every movement, leaving her increasingly unsettled. His gaze was locked on her face, captivated. Another smile tugged at his lips. For a moment, she wondered how it would feel to be close to him and to feel his touch. Suddenly, she snapped out of it and flinched as he started to touch her on parts of her body. He started putting his hand between her legs. She felt she was being punished for her wrongs. She let out a groan and cried out. She plucked enough courage to withdraw herself from him. But as she got to her feet, he would lunge out at her and pull her hair. The little girl's feelings towards her Father were complex and deeply conflicted. She struggled to reconcile the love and trust she had for him as her Father with the fear and anguish caused by his abusive actions. At times, she felt a deep sense of betrayal and confusion, wondering how someone who was supposed to protect and care for her could instead inflict such pain and trauma.

Her Father's actions had shattered her sense of safety and security, leaving her with a profound sense of vulnerability and mistrust. Despite the turmoil and fear he had caused, there were moments when she longed for his love and approval, yearning for the comfort of a nurturing and supportive Father-daughter relationship.

The internal conflict between her cherished memories of her Father's affection and the trauma caused by his abuse created a turbulent emotional landscape for the little girl. She grappled with anger, sorrow, and yearning for a sense of normality that seemed increasingly out of reach.

Ultimately, her journey involved navigating the complex emotions surrounding her Father, seeking healing and understanding while striving to find a path towards forgiveness and inner peace. While enduring the ordeal, she steadfastly visualised Jesus standing by her side. He had repeatedly expressed his love for her, offering comfort by holding her hand and guiding her through difficult times. Yet, he was nowhere to be found when she needed him the most.

The relentless torment persisted, engulfing her, as she questioned Jesus's absence. Did he forget about her? But then, at that moment, she felt his hand placed trustingly into hers. With a gravely earnest expression, she looked up at him, finding solace in his presence. She was safe once more.

She continued on her way, and as she strolled, she came across a towering mountain that captured her. The mountain that emerged on the horizon was shrouded in mist, its peaks reaching towards the sky like the jagged edges of a giant's castle. The dense forest covering the slopes gave the mountain a lush, vibrant green hue, contrasting starkly with the grey cliffs that jutted from its base. The mountain loomed larger and larger, a symbol of both danger and potential refuge. The sight of the mountain stirred a mix of apprehension and hope in the young girl as she pondered what new challenges and possibilities lay ahead. Its presence seemed to hold a mysterious allure, drawing her gaze and kindling a flicker of determination as she braced herself for the uncertain journey on the other side. She confidently ascended to discover what awaited her at the peak. The ascent was arduous, yet with each step, she found a secure handhold, empowered by an inner strength, knowing that Jesus was again by her side. Despite Fear being her most significant limitation, she summoned the courage to proceed. The initial part of the climb was relatively easy, but as she ascended towards the peak, the challenge intensified, making the journey more arduous.

The challenging task ahead of her involved navigating through a narrow passage surrounded by towering rocks. Despite the daunting terrain, she resolutely pressed on, driven by her determination to reach the summit. Her ultimate goal was to behold the serene waters far below, glistening in the sunlight. As she ascended, she encountered a stunning sight. Peering down from the mountainside, "She was greeted" with a mesmerising view of the sapphire-blue sea. Around her, every tree and bush was adorned with vibrant, fragrant petals, creating a tapestry of colour. The entire area was blanketed in a carpet of flowers, offering her the perfect solitude. A serene smile graced her face as she settled down to absorb the picturesque scene, a sense of tranquillity washing over her. She would continue to replay this scene in her mind during many sleepless nights.

The darkness of the night descended rapidly, shrouding everything in its inky cloak. On this particular night, she noticed a fundamental shift in the atmosphere. The trees whispered to each other with a continuous rustling as if bracing themselves for an impending storm. A sense of foreboding crept over her, causing her heart to quicken its pace, primed for flight at a moment's notice. The sky was suddenly illuminated as lightning flashed across it, immediately prompting her to look upward. In that instant, she experienced a distinct sensation of someone's presence and detected subtle movement from behind the rocks. The subsequent flash of lightning was even more intense, resembling the warm glow of copper. The trees shook their leaves fiercely and shivered all their branches. The man emerged deliberately from behind the rock, extending his hand commandingly. "Follow me," he instructed. She took his hand and followed without hesitation, and then a small square wall materialised in front of her, standing about 10 feet high and 6 feet wide.

A small door stood ajar, inviting her curiosity. She cautiously looked through the open door, wondering what she was expecting. There was a green path that led to a small bridge. As she gazed through the door frame, the landscape unfolded like an unfamiliar painting, captivating in its beauty and mystery. Stepping through would mean entering a realm of unbounded possibilities. As she hurried towards it, it seemed to recede into the distance. Perhaps she was dreaming, but it felt entirely natural. It felt as if something or someone was pulling her back. Eyes seemed to peer at her from all directions, full of cruelty. Then, she noticed a faint glimmer of light, giving her the courage to move forward. Although the door was wide open, She persisted in being pulled in the opposite direction.

She felt the eyes glaring at her. She heard laughter and felt herself drawn towards it. Once again, it was her Father laughing with clenched fists. His face grew taut, and he slowly opened his mouth to shout. Once again, she was filled with Fear. "He's going to hurt me again," she whispered, her eyes wide with dread. Her Father took a deep breath, his face turning red with anger. After a tense silence, he shouted at her, his fists clenched and shaking. Tears welled in her eyes and rolled down her cheeks as his face drew closer to hers. She wiped away the tears that streamed down her cheeks, feeling the warmth of his breath against her skin and the dampness of his open mouth. As she drew a deep breath, she mustered the strength to utter, "Go away, leave me alone." The little girl's inner thoughts towards her Father were a tumultuous mix of confusion, fear, and betrayal. Despite the love and guidance she longed for, she couldn't reconcile the abuse she endured at the hands of her Father with the traditional paternal role. There was an internal struggle between her innate desire for safety and the unsettling realization that the person who should provide protection was the source of her turmoil. This conflict gave rise to profound feelings of vulnerability and a yearning for the love and security that a father figure should embody. Yet, amidst the turmoil, there lingered a glimmer of hope and a desperate desire for a loving, fatherly presence that could provide the comfort and reassurance she desperately needed.

Running without direction, she screamed, "No matter where I go, he's always there, causing me pain."

As she fled, her breath came in ragged gasps, and her heart pounded like a drum. Her feet carried her forward, seemingly with a will of their own. Emotions erupted from her heart, setting her soul ablaze with searing intensity. Finally, she collapsed to the ground, her body trembling as tears streamed down her cheeks once more. Jesus' mysterious absence during the moments when her Father caused her deep pain troubled her deeply. She could not shake off the pervasive bewilderment stemming from his absence. Her emotions were a tangled web of confusion, Fear, and a deep-seated sense of being deserted. She found herself wondering why she had to endure such intense suffering alone, feeling isolated and vulnerable. During these moments of torment, she questioned why Jesus seemed distant and disconnected, adding another layer of distress to her already painful experiences.

"The little girl, trembling with Fear and confusion, found herself engulfed in the terrifying presence of her Father, a looming figure emanating anger and hostility. His actions inflicted physical pain but also left deep emotional scars, shattering her sense of security. The absence of support and comfort during these moments of distress emphasised the stark reality of her suffering, highlighting the profound impact of her Father's abusive behaviour on her young life."

"Extend your hand and do not hesitate to seek support, for I possess strength." Upon hearing these words, memories of her Father surged within her. As she lay on the ground, she looked up at Jesus, observing her compassionately. Standing up, straining her eyes to penetrate the pervasive darkness, she noticed a faint glimmer in the distance. The small, twinkling light was the only visible sign of life in the bleak, desolate world around her. Realising that it was the only beacon of hope in that cold, dark expanse, she knew she had no choice but to follow it. As she descended into the night, the once-cool wind began to carry a gentle warmth, and she felt a few raindrops land softly on her face. The air around her grew increasingly humid, and she looked up to see dark, brooding clouds gathering overhead, casting the surroundings in shadow. The sky erupted with lightning, illuminating the dark clouds before the rain poured down in torrents. She urgently sought shelter as the night rapidly descended around her. As she followed the dim glow of light, slowly piercing through the surrounding darkness, her eyes caught sight of a minor, solitary hut nestled in the distance.

The sky above had transformed into a brooding canvas of dark, swirling clouds, signalling an imminent storm. Overwhelmed by unease, she strained to peer through the cascading sheets of rain toward the elusive sanctuary. The repeated reverberations of thunder and the sharp cracks of lightning intensified her anxiety as she hastened her escape, driven by the desperate need to seek shelter within the confines of the remote hut.

The hut provided protection, yet she felt impending danger nearby. The hut had long been deserted, but it offered her protection against the elements. The hut was a small, ramshackle structure with weathered wooden walls that seemed to lean inwards. The thatched roof was patchy and appeared to be on the verge of collapse. The windows, covered in grime, barely let in any light, casting the interior in a murky gloom. The floor was littered with fallen leaves and debris, adding to the sense of neglect and abandonment. The overall atmosphere was one of desolation and decay. The moment she pushed open the creaky wooden door and stepped into the dimly lit hut, a musty smell enveloped her.

Cobwebs clung to every surface, stretching from the rafters to the rusted furniture.

The uneasy feeling in her stomach grew as she took in the eerie scene before her. She stood for a while, glad to be out of the storm. She casually gazed out of one of the windows as a faint sound caught her attention. A tingling sensation of someone's presence outside sent shivers down her spine. With trepidation, she mustered the courage to peer around the corner cautiously. Her muscles tensed and coiled like tightly wound springs, reflecting the mix of anxiety and anticipation coursing through her body. She could feel the adrenaline surging through her, heightening her senses and preparing her for whatever was coming.

She gazed upon a solitary figure standing amidst the tumultuous storm. It was Jesus who stood before her, his hands outstretched. As his fingers moved, the angry clouds above transformed with subtle shifts in colour, as if he were orchestrating the storm like a conductor leading an orchestra. With a grand sweep of his arms, he calmed the turbulent sky. Then, turning his face towards her, he offered a gentle smile.

When she saw Jesus again, she felt an overwhelming sense of peace and comfort, which allowed her to sleep despite feeling exhausted. His presence gave her a deep understanding of security and reassurance, enabling her to find solace and peace. Jesus' unwavering love and support helped her overcome exhaustion and get the rest she needed.

Chapter 5: The Path to Healing

As the morning sunlight filtered through the windows, she stirred from her slumber, desperate for warmth and shelter. Peering out the door, she was astonished to realise she was again facing the same imposing wall she had encountered. She delicately traced her fingers along the rough, weathered stone walls until her hands finally met the excellent, smooth surface of the partially ajar door. As she pushed it open and stepped inside, the darkness enveloped her like a thick, heavy blanket. In that instant, a surge of electrical energy coursed through her body, momentarily causing her to forget the pain and trauma she had endured. Her heart skipped a beat in response to the profound sense of peace and serenity that washed over her. The scene before her was Nothing short of breathtaking. She found a serene spot and settled in, taking in the stunning beauty surrounding her. As she sat there, the vibrant colours of nature brought a rosy glow back to her pale cheeks. Once more, she found herself captivated by the sight of the bridge, and she slowly began to make her way towards it, savouring every step.

Her heart had yearned for this precise moment for an eternity. With unwavering confidence, she traversed, utterly enchanted by the otherworldly elegance of the crystal-laden landscape. The bridge stood in the distance, its arches reaching gracefully across the tranquil river. The soft sunlight bathed the bridge warmly, casting long shadows on the water below. It symbolises a passage from turmoil to peace, a connection between the tumultuous past and the serene present. As she gazed at the bridge, a sense of hope and reconciliation washed over her, as if the bridge held the promise of healing and restoration. She set herself down as she finally reached the bridge and gazed at the clear crystal water below. Had she finally found peace, or was it just for a while? She sat quietly by the edge of the river, feeling the cool breeze on her face as she gazed at the gentle flow of the water. Suddenly, her peaceful moment was interrupted by a soft, pale yellow light streaming across the sky, casting a warm glow over the surroundings. The breathtaking twinkling lights danced and intertwined above the serene, glimmering waters. While it was a truly magical sight, she couldn't help but wonder if she was mistaken in thinking everything seemed as perfect.

She felt overwhelmed and despondent, questioning how much more she could endure. The weight of her struggles had taken its toll, and she was unsure of her ability to persevere. As time passed, the billowing clouds intertwined and gradually obscured the sun's warm rays. A sense of unsettling tranquillity settled over her as she pondered how many more challenges she could withstand. The sky overhead gradually transitioned to a significant greyness for approximately an hour. A substantial mass of grey-white fog moved exceptionally across the water at an extraordinary speed. Emerging from the mist was the unmistakable figure of her Father. At that moment, apprehension gripped her as the realisation dawned that he intended to cause her harm once more.

As she stood frozen in Fear, she watched with mounting horror as he ominously advanced towards her. His angry voice pierced the air, shouting commands that sent shivers down her spine. His gaunt face loomed above her, casting a menacing shadow as he glared at her. Their eyes locked in a chilling gaze, and his steel blue eyes dulled into hers, causing her to instinctively shrink back to evade his intimidating presence. Despite her desperate search for an escape route, she found herself trapped with no way out. He advanced, and suddenly, his hand grabbed hold of her arm, dragging her along the ground, and then he struck her with a savage blow. She recoiled in horror as she fell to the ground. With her instinct kicking in, she attempted to take charge of the situation. Everything seemed to slow down as she somehow found the strength to break free from his grasp. She tumbled to the floor, desperately clutching her head with both hands.

The grip of Fear constricted around her as she cautiously inched along the ground. With each careful movement, she knew that swift action was critical for her survival once more. Breath held, she strained to hear the sound of his approaching footsteps. In her fervent attempt to defend herself, Once again, the young girl found herself gazing into her Father's disconcerting eyes.

Her blood turned icy as he pointed his finger at her, slowly raised his hand, and unleashed swirling coils of power that came writhing towards her. But before she could avoid his advance, his power swirled around her and encircled her tiny body. She began to whimper, and suddenly, a bolt of lightning streaked towards her, and she was frozen rigid with Fear again. She stared intently. as he approached her once again, her small, delicate hands outstretched toward him in eager anticipation; she fought hard to resist his powerful advances towards her, which were paralysing her limbs, but try as she could, she couldn't break free from his grip, and she began to whimper like a frightened puppy. As he struck her, she shuddered and crashed to the ground. He hesitated for a brief moment, torn between retreating and advancing. Ultimately, he lumbered toward her again, and she once again fell to the floor.

The little girl felt a deep sense of Fear, pain, and betrayal when her abusive Father left her on the ground. She was overwhelmed by the physical and emotional pain of the experience, feeling a profound sense of abandonment and vulnerability. The trauma of his actions left her shaken and distraught, struggling to comprehend why her Father would treat her in such a cruel manner. She felt a mix of confusion, Fear, and intense emotional pain as she grappled with the aftermath of his actions. The experience shaped her perceptions of trust, safety, and love. The little girl felt a mix of Fear, confusion, and pain as she fell to the ground. She was overwhelmed by the suddenness of her fall and the impact it had on her tiny body. Confusion clouded her mind as she tried to understand what had happened, and she felt a sharp surge of pain as she hit the ground. Tears filled her eyes as she grappled with the rush of emotions, leaving her feeling vulnerable and frightened. The experience left her longing for comfort and safety, yearning for someone to help her understand what had just occurred. Where was Jesus? The little girl felt a profound loneliness and confusion when she felt that Jesus wasn't there. As she grappled with her emotions, she found herself struggling to understand why she didn't experience the reassuring presence of love and comfort that she had always associated with Jesus. This absence left her vulnerable and lost, longing for the peace and reassurance she hoped to find in her faith.

Chapter 6: Discovering Inner Strength

The sun rose on a new day, but she felt utterly solitary. Her emotions were a tangled mess after the confrontation with her Father the day before. She felt overwhelmed by the weight of the abuse she had endured, unsure if she could bear any more. Upon awakening, the presence of a brilliant white light initially led her to believe that a new day had dawned. Despite her somewhat impaired vision, the light revealed a shimmering, distorted perspective of the trail ahead. Following the meandering path parallel to the river's downstream flow, she deliberated on whether she should venture forth. After careful consideration, she pursued the trail, hoping to locate a safe crossing point. She sought refuge and safety from the harrowing ordeal she had endured with her deeply abusive Father the previous night. She decisively identified a suitable crossing point, carefully observing the area for a few minutes. Confident that it was safe to proceed, she boldly began to cross. A sudden sense of someone's presence made her whirl around as she made her way across the water. Expecting to see her Father, she was surprised to come face to face with the reflection of a young teenage girl - herself - in the water. The face in the reflection was devoid of expression, staring back at her with an eerie blankness.

As a young girl, she was filled with innocence and vulnerability. The trauma of her experiences with her Father left her feeling scared and tearful. She longed for love and security, but instead, she had to navigate through the turmoil caused by her Father's abusive actions. Despite her challenges, she displayed resilience and a longing for peace and security. Her journey was marked by a deep emotional struggle and a yearning for comfort, making her eventual discovery of solace and strength in her faith all the more meaningful. Throughout her formative years, the impact of her Father's actions lingered, shaping her emotional landscape and fostering a deep sense of Fear and insecurity. However, her connection with Jesus gave her the strength to confront her fears and find inner peace. Her journey was defined by her willingness to confront the emotional turmoil caused by her Father's actions and ultimately find peace and security through her faith. Arduous and fatiguing, leaving her harbouring concerns for her safety while mindful of the considerable distance yet to be covered. Despite these challenges, she proceeded forward with determination. She pressed on, her steps wary and deliberate. The path had been anything but straightforward, and now she found herself standing in a quiet square. A weathered signpost, its wooden frame worn and splintered, gestured towards three separate exits. Her eyes flickered from one direction to another, contemplating which path to embark. She hesitated, contemplating her next move, when something caught her attention in the dimly lit surroundings. Emerging from the shadows was a pale-skinned woman, and her piercing eyes held the young woman in an inexplicable trance, rendering her incapable of movement. It dawned on her that it was her Mummy once again. A commanding presence took hold as her Mummy advanced and seized her shoulder.

She felt her Mother's desperate urge to confide something about her Father, yet there was an unmistakable sense of Fear as she struggled to divulge something about herself. As she attempted to discuss her Father, her Mother's demeanour became increasingly evident. She appeared grappling with conflicting emotions as she tried to share her behaviour. Her demeanour showed a subtle shift, indicating that she harboured deeper feelings than she expressed. She was torn between safeguarding her family and disclosing the truth about her Father's actions. It's difficult to say precisely how her Mummy felt during that storm. One can only imagine that she was likely experiencing emotional turmoil, potentially feeling a sense of helplessness and Fear for her child's safety. Her lack of response to her daughter's pleas may have been due to being overwhelmed by the situation or feeling powerless to provide the comfort and reassurance her daughter needed. It's possible that her Mummy was also dealing with her emotional challenges, which could have made it difficult for her to support her daughter during such a frightening experience effectively.

Then, a dark, indistinct figure emerged from the shadows behind her. It was her Father once again. A shiver ran down her spine, a foreboding sense of danger enveloping her, accompanied by a tingling sensation as if a horde of spiders were crawling from her shoulder to the nape of her neck. Her Mother was taken aback, her eyes widening in surprise as she instinctively stepped backwards in response to his unexpected appearance. She, too, felt a surge of Fear, causing the young girl to be visibly startled. Why! Was she afraid? The Mother's Fear of her Father could be attributed to her own experiences with him, which might have been characterised by intimidation and abuse. This Fear could have stemmed from the Father's domineering and threatening behaviour, creating an atmosphere of Fear and insecurity for the Mother and the daughter. When her Father emerged the little girl felt a sense of comfort wash over her as her Mummy gave her a reassuring smile, easing her worries and making her feel safe. A weighty silence fell upon them. Standing in silence, they both turned away and at that moment, her Mother directed a tender and reassuring smile back at her daughter, which served as an unspoken promise that everything would be alright. The little girl felt a sense of comfort wash over her as her mommy gave her a reassuring smile, easing her worries and making her feel safe. The little girl's feelings towards her mother underwent a profound shift when she discovered that her mother was also being abused. The realization brought many emotions, including empathy, sorrow, and a deep sense of shared vulnerability. The revelation created a deep understanding and compassion for the young girl, as she recognized her mother's immense strength and resilience while enduring similar hardships. This newfound understanding fostered a profound bond of empathy and solidarity between the two, strengthening their connection as they navigated through their shared experiences of abuse. She continued her journey through the picturesque landscape, carefully scrutinising the directions on the signpost that led her to the third exit. Contemplating the potential destinations awaiting her, she steadily advanced along the natural trail, along the river's edge, taking in the sights and sounds of nature.

As the little girl travelled along the river's edge, she immersed herself in a picturesque landscape. The tranquil flow of the river mirrored the clear, azure sky above, creating a mesmerising reflection of the fluffy white clouds drifting lazily overhead. The verdant greenery lining the riverbanks exuded a lively, vibrant aura, casting a serene and peaceful ambience over the entire scene. The warm and bright sunlight illuminated the surroundings, creating a radiant and enchanting atmosphere. The landscape became golden, illuminating the surrounding trees and casting enchanting, dancing shadows upon the rippling water. With each bend in the river, the girl found herself enveloped in the serene beauty of nature, providing a soothing sense of peace and tranquillity throughout her journey. Her weariness weighed heavily on her, and she noticed tiny, flickering points of light rapidly darting past her nearly closed eyes. In the distance, faint and muffled sounds barely reached her ears through the piercing howl of the wind as she gradually opened her eyes. She needed to take a break, find time to rest, and recharge her energy. As she sat there, the figure of Jesus came into her line of sight. Dazed, she staggered and shook her head, attempting to dispel the haziness clouding her vision. At that moment, all the love within her young, weary body poured out towards him, evoking a flood of memories rushing back all at once. She enveloped him in her embrace, and she sobbed uncontrollably. The more she tried to hold back her tears, the more they poured out. In that moment of shared grief, they stood together, isolated from the world, seeking solace in each other as their tears mingled, a physical manifestation of their shared pain." Please don't leave me, Jesus," she sobbed, clinging to him. Resting her head on his shoulder, he began to sway her gently. She held on to him tightly, a small tear trickling down her nose and falling onto Jesus's face. Eventually, she drifted off to sleep.

Chapter 7: A Journey of Faith

When she saw Jesus the following day, she felt a profound sense of relief and comfort. It was as if all her worries and troubles had melted away in his presence. Her heart was filled with joy and peace, and she felt overwhelming love and compassion emanating from him. The radiant look in his eyes seemed to envelop her in a warm embrace, and she couldn't help but glow with happiness as she gazed into his eyes. Opening her eyes and seeing Jesus there, her heart swelled with indescribable joy. It was as if all her longings, doubts, and fears disappeared instantly. A profound sense of peace washed over her, and her whole being was filled with warmth and reassurance. At that moment, she felt an overwhelming sense of love and comfort, as if all the pieces of her life had finally fallen into place. The landscape unfolded before them in a grand display of nature's beauty, leaving them in awe. As she walked alongside Jesus, the trail led them through a breathtaking panorama. The tranquil river flowed gently beside them, reflecting the warm sunlight and adding to the scene's serenity. It was a profoundly comforting and peaceful experience to be surrounded by such stunning natural beauty with Jesus by her side. Amidst the beauty, she tenderly reached out and placed her hand in his, feeling a profound sense of comfort and deep companionship. The trail they followed ran along the river's edge, offering exceptional views of the surrounding natural beauty. Despite the day's challenges, she found comfort in the unwavering support of Jesus, who accompanied her every step. They leisurely wandered along the winding trail until they found themselves beneath the sheltering canopy of a cluster of trees.

As she gazed about, a scattering of sunbeams pierced through the leaves, enveloping her in a comforting, golden radiance. As the hours passed and the brassy sun descended towards the horizon, a deepening frown etched above her eyes. She was acutely aware of how rapidly the night would envelop her once the sun dipped below the horizon. As the night fell, it engulfed her in its hostile and dark embrace. She lazily observed the flickering shadows dancing around her, only to find that Jesus had suddenly vanished. The slow dripping of moisture from the trees created a hauntingly rhythmic soundtrack. Then, a fog swiftly descended upon the hilltops, draping the landscape in a thick, white curtain that obscured the water below. As she gazed into the dense fog, a faint light emerged, swaying and weaving its way towards her. The light didn't follow a straight path but moved from side to side as if dancing on the water's surface. Amidst the eerie scene, she could hear the faint, haunting sounds of singing drifting towards her. The singing sounds were eerie yet beautiful as if echoing from a distant, otherworldly realm. The haunting melody carried an indescribable mix of sorrow and longing, captivating her senses and sending shivers down her spine. Her surroundings were engulfed in a bright light, swirling and rushing around her at an increasing speed. The sky emanated a golden glow, and she observed the water shimmering with changing colours as the light slowly faded, making way for the stars. When she found herself concealed within the shadows, she came to a sudden halt and stood perfectly motionless, taking in all the sounds surrounding her. The sudden burst of light startled her, briefly illuminating her Father's concerned face before the glare forced her to shut her eyes. As the world plunged into darkness, she felt disoriented. When she tentatively reopened her eyes, she found herself in an unfamiliar place, disoriented and unsure of her surroundings.

"Child, do you know where you are?" The voice seemed to come from afar. She saw Jesus, but her Mummy and Father were standing over her. The young girl was confused and surprised when her Father told her everything she had experienced was a dream. She struggled to comprehend how her vivid experiences could be just a dream. It felt like the ground had slipped under her feet, leaving her uncertain. "Oh no, where am I? How did I get here?" she asked weakly as her Father stood before her. Her Father stepped forward, saying, "You've been dreaming." But it all felt natural to her; could it have been a dream? The little girl struggled to accept that it had all been a dream. She found it difficult to reconcile the vividness and realness of her experiences with the notion that they were all just a creation of her mind. It felt unsettling to consider that everything she had felt and experienced was unreal, leaving her confused and uncertain. She was in a partially lit room, gazing at the ceiling above her head. It looked strangely white in the dark room. The room that the little girl found herself in resembled a place of gloom and despair. It was dimly lit by a single flickering lamp, casting eerie shadows on the worn and neglected furniture. The heavy curtains drawn over the windows made the atmosphere feel even more oppressive, and the bare, uninspiring walls added to the sense of Fear and isolation. The room was dimly lit as she gazed around. Suddenly, the play of light formed an intricate picture on the wall - a breathtaking waterfall scene. At that moment, she felt the tears welling up, unable to resist the overwhelming surge of emotion.

The little girl found herself in this room as a refuge from the chaos and noise outside. The image of the waterfall brought her peace and tranquillity, yet simultaneously, it stirred up emotions she had been holding back. It meant she was on the verge of releasing pent-up feelings and finding solace amid her inner turmoil. The stark realisation washed over her like a cold wave crashing against the shore. She couldn't deny the overwhelming realisation that the suffering she endured was not just a product of her imagination, but a cruel manifestation of the trauma inflicted upon her by her Father. His dismissive statement that it was all a dream starkly contrasted with the truth. He held power over not only her physical well-being but also her emotions. Her tears cascaded down her cheeks, resembling large, shimmering drops as they splashed into the glistening waterfall below. Tears streamed down her cheeks, and she wiped them away hastily, but more kept flowing. There was something unusual about these tears. Unlike the familiar anger that accompanied her previous tears, this time, they felt different, stirring a mix of emotions within her. They were truly uplifted. Her overflowing happiness was contagious as she sang and danced, entirely free from tears. Her senses became keenly aware of Jesus's profound presence as he gently touched her. The little girl felt a mixture of confusion and vulnerability about her tears. At times, she was overwhelmed by the torrent of emotions that accompanied her tears, feeling as though they exposed her deepest fears and insecurities. Her tears served as a tangible manifestation of the turmoil within her, often leaving her feeling exposed and raw. However, as she found solace and comfort in her growing connection and love for Jesus, her Perception of her tears began to shift. She started to view her tears not as a sign of weakness but as a release of the overwhelming emotions that had weighed heavily on her young heart. In the quiet moments of reflection, she saw her tears as a path to healing, a cleansing of the pain that had overshadowed her childhood, and a means to embrace the possibility of inner peace and renewal— touched her head. As her tears streamed down, it felt as though they were cleansing away all the pain and hardship she had endured. The feelings she experienced when Jesus was there were indescribable. It was as if a warm blanket had been wrapped around her, filling her with a sense of safety and comfort. The overwhelming love and peace that enveloped her in those moments made her feel she could overcome anything. The presence of Jesus gave her the strength to confront her fears and provided a refuge from the storm that had raged within her for so long. In those moments, she found a sense of security and serenity that she had longed for, and it gave her the hope and resilience to move forward on her journey towards healing and peace. As she knelt before Jesus, a rush of happiness swept over her, engulfing her in a sea of joy. She poured out her love for him, knowing that he also loved her as his child. She lowered her head as she knelt, allowing her long hair to fall and obscure her face. In the background, her Father's voice could be heard, angrily shouting at her, "Sit up and look at me." Despite his demands, she remained focused on Jesus, not daring to meet her Father's gaze. An angry figure, her Father, loomed over her, but she transformed his harsh voice into the soothing sound of water bubbling through stones. At that moment, she found solace in the knowledge that she was completely safe in the presence of Jesus. As she reflected, she embraced the thought, "I am alright now," fully aware that she must cling to this belief amidst the ongoing storms she was bound to encounter. Her complex emotions towards her Father lingered, and she held the certainty that this fleeting peace would not persist indefinitely. A radiant light illuminated her heart and mind, clarifying many things. That night, she prayed, pouring her heart out to Jesus.

Chapter 8: Finding Solace

A profound change filled the air as she awoke to the soft morning light. The gentle rays of sunlight seemed to bring a serene peace, and the cheerful symphony of birdsong matched the tranquillity she felt in her heart. It was as if a new understanding had blossomed within her, realising that she had weathered the storm and emerged in deep serenity. She greeted the day ahead with renewed purpose, hope, and unwavering faith. As she stood up, the excitement gradually faded, like air escaping from a balloon. Once again, she found herself face to face with her Mummy and Father, their expressions quickly replacing the fleeting joy with a sobering reality. The little girl's heart raced as she caught sight of her Mother and Father. Her Mother's warm smile and outstretched arms brought a flicker of hope into her heart. As she rushed into her embrace, she felt a sense of security washing over her, momentarily calming the storm of emotions.

In contrast, her Father's presence cast a shadow of Fear and apprehension. The memory of his intimidating figure and past actions left her trembling as she struggled to reconcile his earthly role with her yearning for a loving and protective father. As her Father slowly approached her, she glanced around and settled her eyes on a door tucked in the corner. Upon opening the door, she felt a rush of emotions flooding her senses. Anxious anticipation mingled with a glimmer of hope as she stepped into the unknown. Each door creak echoed like a heartbeat, resonating with excitement and trepidation. She braced herself for whatever lay on the other side, embracing the uncertainty with a newfound courage. The door was made of solid oak, and its rich, dark grain added character to its surface. The brass doorknob gleamed in the soft light, inviting anyone to grasp it and uncover the mysteries that lay beyond. As her fingers wrapped around the handle, the intricate carvings on the door seemed to come to life, telling a story of elegance and history etched into its very surface. The door swung open, unveiling a realm of endless possibilities, accompanied by the haunting echoes of its creaking hinges as if beckoning her to step into the unknown. With measured, tentative steps, she edged closer, her heart filled with anticipation to unravel the mysteries beyond. She constantly sensed the weight of her Father's gaze upon her, as if his eyes never left her side.

As she pushed the heavy door, it creaked open, enveloping her in complete darkness. A sudden chill descended, and a fine drizzle prickled her skin. She shuddered as she made out the outline of a flight of steps materialising in front of her. As she gazed upon the flight of steps, a wave of uncertainty washed over her, mingling with a formidable sense of determination. Each step seemed to stretch out endlessly before her, prompting her to carefully contemplate the journey ahead while acknowledging the need for attentiveness and care at every stage of the descent. She carefully felt her way along, slowly beginning to descend the stairs. With each step, she reached out, her hand brushing the space in front of her to ensure she didn't collide with anything. The steps led her into the darkness, and she was unsure of what lay beyond. However, she knew that her cautious descent would eventually reveal the destination at the bottom of the stairs. The spiral staircase seemed to stretch endlessly downward as she descended, the darkness enveloping her with each step. After what felt like an eternity, a dim, grey light appeared, offering a glimmer of hope in the oppressive darkness. The stairs ultimately led to a flat, seemingly endless passage stretching before her. Abruptly, she froze, straining to listen as the sound of descending footsteps echoed ominously. Her heart pounded in terror as she couldn't shake the feeling that someone, or something, was following closely behind her, adding to the growing sense of dread and anxiety.

"Could it have been her Father? The silence was broken only by the sharp intake of her breath as a man's voice boomed her name, followed by a woman's voice joining in, echoing and repeating her name repeatedly. The volume of the voices began to intensify, creating a sense of impending closeness. A deep, hostile growl emanated from a male voice, while a distressed moan mingled with it from a female voice. It was unmistakably her Father and Mother. The surrounding voices cascaded, amplifying in volume and proximity, reverberating through the air. Within this chorus, she immediately discerned the hostility in the male voice and the distress in the female voice, identifying them as her Father and Mother. When she finally recognised that it was her Mummy and Father, a whirlwind of emotions swirled inside her. There was a strange mix of relief, Fear, and confusion. The memories of her Father's abusive actions and her Mother's perceived distance and frailty flooded her mind, intensifying her conflicting emotions. She longed for her Mother's comforting embrace, yet she also felt a deep sense of Fear and insecurity due to her Father's past actions. It was a moment filled with a complex array of emotions, reflecting the profound impact of her past experiences on her present perceptions and feelings. She shivered as an icy chill enveloped her, and in the distance, she could hear the rising wind, its mournful howl carrying a sense of foreboding. It felt like a door to some forbidden landscape had been abruptly blown open. The sound of the wind intensified, drowning out her parents' voices, and the piercing echo of the wind swallowed her name as they vanished into the turbulent gusts. She started walking along the passage, which stretched for miles. She couldn't help but wonder where it would lead her. Suddenly, bone-chilling water started to encircle her knees. There was Nothing to do but go forward. "I have to get through this," she thought, quickening her pace. The icy water crept up to her waist now. She moved like an overweighted deep-sea diver, with water now lapping very quickly around her neck. She twisted her head upwards and to the side, struggling to keep breathing. If the water gets any deeper, I won't make it. She felt a flood of frustration as she came to the sudden realisation that there was no possibility of reaching higher ground. She leaned against the water. Time and time again, her feet slipped, and she grabbed at a rock ceiling less than a foot above her for support. The tunnel seemed to stretch endlessly before her, engulfed in an ominous darkness that seemed to suffocate any glimmer of light. As she navigated through the claustrophobic confines of the tunnel, the walls pressed in on her, amplifying her sense of confinement and dread. Each step felt like a struggle against an invisible force pulling her deeper into the darkness.

The weight of the water pressed against her chest, making it difficult to draw breath, and the sound of her frantic heartbeat echoed in her ears. Panic surged through her veins as she fought against the relentless pull of the water, her limbs growing heavy with exhaustion.

Her mind raced with thoughts of desperation and Fear, the cold grip of the water seeping into her bones. As she struggled to find an escape, a sense of overwhelming helplessness enveloped her, and the tunnel felt like an inescapable prison, drowning her in a relentless tide of terror and despair. As she continued navigating through the tunnel, a wave of discomfort engulfed her, causing her back to stiffen and her legs to throb. Each step felt like an immense struggle, and a growing sense of frustration and exhaustion made the journey even more challenging. However, relief washed over her after an interminable period as she detected a subtle incline in the tunnel. Despite her aching body, the realisation that progress was being made filled her with renewed determination and hope. Her hands trembled as she desperately clawed her way upward, her face drenched in a cold sweat. A chilling wind swept through the tunnel, creating an eerie symphony of swirling and whistling around her. Finally, she emerged through an opening at the top, but where had she arrived? She rested on the surface, waiting for her breathing to steady, unsure of what lay ahead. Once again, tears welled in her eyes. Initially, her emotion stemmed from sheer gratitude for being alive. Her battles for survival were to begin again. Words turned around in her mind. She knew she must face up to all the storms that she would have to go through. The young girl has been through intense battles that have left deep emotional and psychological scars. She experienced sexual abuse at a very young age, causing her tremendous Fear and turmoil. These experiences impacted her deeply, pushing her into a stormy and tumultuous existence. The memories of the abuse made her feel scared and tearful, and she longed for love and security that seemed out of reach.

The battles she has faced include inner turmoil, Fear, vulnerability, and a profound sense of isolation. The storm she weathered in the boat symbolised the chaos and fear she felt within herself, heightened by the overwhelming darkness and the relentless crashing of the waves. Her unmet longing for security and comfort intensified her emotions, leaving her adrift in a sea of uncertainty and Fear. During the raging storm, the young girl found solace in memories of comfort and love, weaving them into a protective cocoon that shielded her from the relentless onslaught. She drew upon the gentle warmth of her mother's embrace, conjuring vivid recollections of soothing lullabies and tender caresses that enveloped her in a blanket of reassurance.

As the tempest raged, she clung to these memories, allowing them to form an ethereal shield against the storm's ferocity. In her mind, she revisited moments of unwavering love and unwavering faith, allowing their radiance to permeate the darkness that threatened to engulf her. These memories became a beacon of hope amidst the chaos, illuminating her path with the tender glow of cherished experiences and heartfelt gestures of kindness.

With each crashing wave and thunderous roar, she held onto these memories like precious fragments of light, weaving them into an invisible armour that gave her comfort and security. They became her sanctuary in the tumultuous sea of emotions, offering a respite from the turmoil and instilling within her a steadfast resolve.

The girl was cocooned in love and serenity in these moments, fortified by the enduring embrace of cherished memories. They became her anchor amidst the storm, shielding her from the relentless tempest and infusing her with a quiet strength that transcended the tumultuous forces that sought to overwhelm her.

As the girl weathered the storm, she discovered that the love and comfort she held within her heart became an unyielding fortress, offering refuge from the chaos and empowering her to navigate the turbulent waters with grace and unwavering resilience.

Despite her tumultuous challenges, her resilience has shone through, offering a glimpse of inner strength that will eventually guide her toward healing and peace. In a moment of clarity, she realised that Jesus was by her side, offering comfort and support. With the presence of Jesus, she held onto hope, believing that she would emerge from this experience as a more robust and better person. The song "Footprints" paints a vivid picture of a man reflecting on his life as he gazes at two sets of footprints, one belonging to himself and the other to God, etched across a vast beach. At times, one of the footprints mysteriously vanishes, prompting the man to question why he was seemingly abandoned during his most trying moments. In response, Jesus reassures him, explaining that when only one set of footprints is visible during his times of suffering and hardship, it was because He was carrying the man through those challenging times. The little girl found solace and reflection in the song "Footprints in the Sand" as she faced the storms. The song's lyrics resonated deeply with her as she navigated through tumultuous times, much like a storm at sea. The image of footprints alongside her during the most challenging moments served as a source of comfort and hope. It reminded her she was not alone, even in the darkest and most difficult times. The song became a powerful reminder of inner strength and the presence of a guiding force, helping her endure the storms and find a path towards healing and peace. She was to remember this as her battles continued throughout her life.

Chapter 9: Rays Of Hope

As she gazed up, the sun appeared to hang over the horizon as though it was on the verge of being swallowed by the glistening grey waters. Following a day filled with turmoil, she cautiously made her way forward before hastening to a rock, a slender ledge of stone that projected outwards. There, a sense of tranquillity washed over her. The sky was adorned with a scattering of clouds, and the setting sun cast a mesmerising pink hue upon them. Immersed in the moment, she gazed upward, revelling in the rapid and breathtaking transformations unfolding across the sky. The sky was a captivating display of vibrant colours as the sun descended behind the horizon. Shades of pink, orange, and gold painted the heavens, creating a breathtaking tapestry of light and shadow. The clouds seemed to catch fire as they reflected the sun's last rays, casting a warm, ethereal glow across the darkening sky. The dim light gradually faded as she struggled to rise to her knees, feeling utterly exhausted from the previous day's turmoil within the tunnel's confines. As she prepared to leave the shelter of the rock, a sudden flicker of movement caught her eye, drawing her attention back to the water below. Excitedly, she beheld a group of dolphins leaping and frolicking in the fading light. Their elegant forms soared above the water before gracefully plunging back into the depths, their movements a dance of pure joy and freedom. As she stood on the shore, she watched in awe as the acrobatics of the sea created a mesmerising display of ripples spreading across the water. It was her first encounter with the sea's peacefulness, leaving her breathless. This discovery that the sea was not always her adversary felt like a secret glimpse of paradise. The world she had never known unfolded, filling her with wonder and enchantment. So captivated was she by this newfound beauty that she didn't notice someone approaching her. She suddenly turned her head when she felt someone very close to her. It wasn't Jesus, but her Father once again. When their eyes met, they both cried out. She uttered a shrill cry of terror while he roared in fury like a charging bull. He threw himself forward. "Please, don't! Leave me alone," she cried out as she went to the very edge of the ledge, yelling and waving her arms. When her Father approached once again, the little girl felt a mix of Fear, sadness, and anxiety. His presence deeply unsettled her, often bringing intense emotions to the surface. She pondered his intentions as she listened to yet another unidentifiable noise.

A deep, unending roar filled the air, sending shivers of Fear down her spine. Standing frozen in place, she gazed into the distance, trying to discern the source of the mysterious sound. After a moment, realisation struck - it was the sound of a mighty waterfall. The rushing water formed a magnificent curtain between herself and her Father. When she heard the waterfall, she felt Fear and awe. The deep, continuous roar overwhelmed her with dread, but as she recognised the sound for what it was, a feeling of wonder and amazement washed over her. The realisation of the powerful natural force before her frightened and captivated her. The waterfall was a sight to behold. It cascaded down from a great height, its waters forming a glistening curtain stretching endlessly. The sound of its relentless, thundering roar filled the air, creating a powerful and mesmerising sensation. The water rushed over the edge, creating a breathtaking spectacle of nature's raw strength and beauty. The sheer force and energy of the falling water made a misty spray that hung in the air, adding to the dramatic and awe-inspiring scene. It was an overwhelming sight and a mesmerising display of nature's power.

As a fine mist danced in the air, it landed gently on her face, creating a sense of uncertainty within her. Standing still, she grappled with conflicting emotions as her Father drew nearer. It felt like she was sinking into an emotional quicksand; her hands clenched, and her lips stiffened in response to the overwhelming flood of feelings. The quicksand seemed an emotional abyss, pulling the little girl more profoundly into despair and vulnerability. It felt like an all-encompassing force dragging her down. The turmoil within her mirrored the relentless pull of the quicksand, leaving her feeling trapped and overwhelmed. Despite her struggle, she clung to a fragile thread of hope, refusing to be entirely engulfed by the emotional quicksand. She was determined to fight him this time, although she felt weak against her Father.

As she approached the waterfall, his voice was lost in a gasp, drowned out by the enormous spray that enveloped her. She was flung, gasping and helpless, against her Father by the force of the water. For a heartrending moment, she found herself nestled in her Father's comforting embrace, her lips slightly parted, her gaze holding onto him for dear life. Beneath her drenched lashes, his strong arms enveloped her slender body, causing his heart to race delightfully. The sweet desire aroused by their physical nearness overwhelmed him. And then an overpowering fear poured over her. "He began to run his fingers through her hair. She looked at him, forcing her eyes to meet his and not to be drowned by them. "You love me, don't you?" One hand was now unconsciously going over her body. Oh no, what was happening." She lashed out at him, causing him to retreat from her as he gazed at her in astonishment. She was filled with a sense of overwhelming Fear as she struggled to comprehend what had just occurred. As she stood on the rocky ledge, feeling the weight of isolation, she cried out to Jesus. Peering down at the majestic waves crashing below, she was overcome by the power of the sea. However, amidst the churning waters, she didn't just see the rise and fall of waves but the figure of Jesus approaching her. A mixture of emotions washed over her - Despite the sharp pang tugging at her heart, she couldn't help but smile through the sudden blur of tears as she sensed his comforting presence drawing near. As she gazed into the depths of Jesus's eyes, she summoned the strength to grace him with a gallant smile. Her eyes shut swiftly as he gently took hold of her hands. As he spoke to her, the painful expression on her face slowly eased away. "You are precious in my eyes," his voice was incredibly calming. An overwhelming sense of tranquillity consumed her.

Chapter 10: The Healing Process

For many years, this little girl was physically and sexually abused by her Father. During that time, she felt alone and unloved. However, as she grew older, she firmly believed in Jesus. This is her true story of how Jesus revealed his love to her during the difficult times she endured as a child and as an adult.

I vividly picture a young girl seated at the tranquil water's edge as I close my eyes. This serene spot held a profound significance for her. The rhythmic sound of the waves crashing against the rugged rocks gave her solace. Each day, she felt embraced by the warm caress of the sun and the gentle embrace of the waves. It was in this place that she could feel the comforting presence of Jesus. As she realised that Jesus was her healer, a profound sense of relief and hope washed over her. It felt like a heavy burden had been lifted from her shoulders, and for the first time, she experienced a glimmer of peace and inner healing. The love and faith in Jesus filled her with newfound strength, dispelling the Fear and turmoil that had gripped her for so long. It was a transformative moment where she felt overwhelming love and comfort, knowing she was not alone in her struggles. The gentle love of Jesus enveloped her, providing the solace and guidance she had yearned for, and she found the courage to move forward and embrace a path towards healing and restoration. She would gently drift along in the calm water, soaking in the peaceful serenity of the surroundings. However, she encountered many more battles that demanded her attention throughout her adult life. Her childhood memories of enduring abuse at the hands of her Father gradually became shrouded in a heavy blanket of depression. She grappled with feelings of responsibility for everything that had occurred, with overwhelming guilt and shame consuming her. At times, she even questioned whether she deserved the pain inflicted by her Father. These emotions were just a glimpse of her internal struggles as she navigated adulthood. She carried the weight of her depression like a suffocating blanket, its heavy layers wrapping around her and making every step feel like an impossible burden. The darkness of her thoughts seemed to swallow her whole, leaving her feeling lost in an unending fog of despair. Each day became a relentless battle against the relentless tide of emotions that threatened to overwhelm her at every turn.

The weight of her past and the heaviness of her present bore down on her, casting a shadow over every aspect of her life. She grappled with profound loneliness, experiencing moments where she felt entrapped in a profound darkness with no apparent means of escape. During these challenging periods, she found she couldn't even see the strength to turn to Jesus, seeking solace amid her profound suffering.

Depression felt like she was being enveloped in a heavy, suffocating fog that dulls every experience and emotion. It was like a weight being pressed down on her chest, making it hard to breathe and draining the colours out of the world. Even the simplest tasks can feel insurmountable, and the future appears devoid of hope or joy. It's like being stuck in a labyrinth with no apparent way out, unable to see beyond the overwhelming darkness surrounding her. Everyday activities can become exhausting, and facing another day feels daunting. Depression made her feel isolated as if she was trapped in a bottomless, dark pit with no way to climb out. In moments of depression, memories from her childhood would rush back to her, overwhelming her with their intensity. In addition, she grappled with the overwhelming feeling of rejection in her childhood.

The little girl then yearned for her Mother's comforting embrace and guidance, but when she called out to her, she sensed an air of distance and frailty about her Mother, who did not respond. This lack of response from her Mother intensified her feelings of rejection. She longed for the warmth and security that a mother's love brings, but the absence of a comforting embrace during such a terrifying experience deepened her sense of abandonment and rejection. The silence that greeted her cries for help echoed her emotional distance from her Mother, accentuating the profound meaning of rejection that lingered in her young heart. This rejection left an indelible mark on her, shaping her Perception of love and security in her formative years. But as time passed, she finally understood why her mother had been so distant. It was then that she learned about the abuse her mother had endured. She realised that her Father had also subjected her to physical and emotional abuse. The way she felt about her mother had undergone a complete transformation as she came to understand the reasons behind her mother's fragility and inability to confront the fact that her child was being abused. Her mother's character was shaped by her own experiences of physical and emotional abuse. She carried herself with a sense of fragility as if she bore the weight of her past on her shoulders. Her eyes held a constant shadow of pain, reflecting the scars left by the tumultuous events she had endured. Despite her hardships, she exuded a quiet strength that resonated in the gentle touch of her hand and the softness of her voice. She often withdrew into herself, seeking refuge in her silent world, where she navigated the lingering turmoil of her past. Her love for her daughter was evident in the tender moments when she sought solace in their bond, offering a comforting presence that transcended words. Though her wounds remained unhealed, she found solace in nurturing her daughter with an enduring love that served as a balm for both their wounded souls. I can only imagine how difficult it must have been for her mother to cope with the knowledge that her child was being abused. She likely felt overwhelmed, helpless, and torn between protecting her child and confronting the reality of the situation. The guilt, Fear, and shock feelings would have been incredibly distressing for her. It's understandable that she may have struggled to accept the situation and felt fragile in dealing with such a challenging and painful reality. When the young adult discovered the abuse her mother had experienced, she felt a surge of conflicting emotions. On one hand, she experienced a deep sense of empathy and sadness for her mother, knowing that she had also gone through a traumatic experience. At the same time, there was a feeling of betrayal and abandonment, as she had looked to her mother for comfort and support in her own time of need. This revelation brought a mix of empathy, understanding, and a complex range of emotions that she needed time to process and come to terms with. Her faith in Jesus, through prayer and seeking spiritual guidance, provided her with a sense of peace and hope. The teachings of Jesus about love and perseverance gave her renewed strength and resilience. Attending the heartfelt church services and immersing herself in worship deepened her profound connection to a higher power, bringing comfort and reassurance. Through her unwavering trust in Jesus and the unwavering support of her church community, she discovered the inner strength to navigate through the depths of her depression and ultimately experience profound healing. After many years of longing, she finally reached the picturesque spot she had always imagined. She settled by the tranquil water's edge with a sense of contentment, just as she had often dreamed. She settled into her seat, her gaze spanning the picturesque landscape. The sky and water shimmered with a golden hue, creating an illusion. As an adult, she was drawn to the water's edge, where a scene of breathtaking serenity unfolded. The rhythmic ebb and flow of the waves created a mesmerising dance, their gentle caress against the shore akin to nature's soothing lullaby. The expansive stretch of crystal-clear water shimmered under the radiant sunlight, reflecting the boundless expanse of the cerulean sky above. After years of turmoil and inner struggle, the young adult stood at the shore, gazing at the calm, glistening waters before her. The memories of the ferocious storm from her childhood still lingered, but a newfound sense of peace and resilience filled her heart. A gentle smile tugged at the corners of her lips as she breathed in the soothing salty air.

With each step she took towards the water, the weight of her past seemed to lift, replaced by a profound sense of healing and hope. As the waves lapped softly against the shore, she felt a deep connection to the tranquillity of the sea, a profound metaphor for the serenity she had found within herself.

Taking a deep breath, she waded into the clear, calm waters, feeling the gentle embrace of the ocean. With each step, she felt the burden of her past lifting, washed away by the tranquil waters surrounding her. And as she submerged herself, she emerged anew, cleansed of the turmoil that had once threatened to engulf her.

As the sunlight danced upon the water's surface, she felt a sense of rebirth, a renewal of spirit and a newfound sense of inner peace. In that moment, she found solace in the calm waters, a testament to her unwavering strength and resilience. With each stroke through the tranquil sea, she embraced the promise of a brighter, hopeful future, knowing she had finally found her way to the calm waters, where healing and tranquillity awaited her.

As she basked in the warmth of the sun's embrace, a profound sense of peace enveloped her, casting a gentle veil over the cares and concerns of everyday life. The whisper of the breeze carried the fragrance of salt and sea, weaving a tapestry of sensory delight around her. With each breath, she felt an exquisite harmony between her inner being and the natural world, as if the very essence of the scene before her resonated with the deepest recesses of her soul, offering solace and rejuvenation. that she was wading knee-deep in a river of gold. As she sat by the water's edge, surrounded by the soft glow of the afternoon light, her mind was suddenly filled with vivid recollections of her childhood. The memories surfaced with a surprising clarity, each bringing a rush of emotion and nostalgia. In this tranquil moment, memories from the past began to resurface, catching her off guard. She had felt a profound sense of complete inner healing. However, she couldn't understand why the memories were resurfacing. Even though she had found healing and peace through her faith in Jesus, the resurfacing of her childhood memories evoked a complex range of emotions within her. She felt a profound sense of vulnerability and Fear as she confronted the painful past. The memories made her feel scared, tearful, and overwhelmed as if she was being pulled back into the storm of her traumatic experiences. Despite her inner turmoil, she also felt a growing sense of resilience and determination, knowing that her faith and the love of Jesus had given her the strength to face these difficult emotions and move forward. The conflicting feelings of Fear and hope intertwined, creating a bittersweet reminder of her journey towards healing and peace. She felt that her experience must have been a significant part of her healing process. As she finds her childhood memories weighing heavily on her mind, she feels a deep longing to seek solace in Jesus to help her navigate through these challenging emotions.

As darkness fell on her again, she felt a familiar sense of unease creeping over her. The encroaching darkness weighed heavily on her shoulders, and she couldn't help but feel lonely. Uncertainty and Fear started to gnaw at the edges of her mind, making her yearn for the comforting embrace of light and warmth. Despite her apprehension, she summoned her inner strength, determined to navigate through the shadows with resilience and courage. Once her eyes adjusted to the darkness, she cast her gaze upwards and was greeted by a mesmerising display. The velvety black expanse was adorned with numerous stars, each twinkling like a precious jewel. Their gentle glow offered hope in the enveloping darkness, painting an enchanting and eerie scene. In desperation, she cried out to Jesus, pleading for his help and searching for an answer as to why she was again experiencing this hardship. She longed for Nothing more than to drift into a peaceful slumber. As sleep slowly overtook her, its arrival was incredibly gentle and comforting. As she succumbed to sleep's embrace, a wave of peacefulness enveloped her, and she anticipated waking up to a renewed sense of energy and clarity. As she entered adulthood, the tranquil imagery of calm waters retained a profound significance for her. The memory of being on calm waters in her dreams remained, evolving into a symbol of resilience, hope, and the unrelenting pursuit of inner peace.

The serene expanse of calm waters became a refuge amidst life's turbulent journey, a reminder that moments of stillness and tranquillity could be discovered amid chaos. It served as an anchor for her, symbolising the strength and resilience she had cultivated through her experiences.

The imagery of calm waters evoked optimism, poignantly reminding us that healing and tranquillity are attainable. It became a powerful metaphor for overcoming adversity, navigating life's storms, and eventually finding a sense of stillness and peace within herself.

In adulthood, the vision of calm waters became an empowering symbol, reminding her that moments of respite and serenity could be found amidst life's challenges. It epitomised her unwavering resilience in adversity and the profound sense of peace she had cultivated over time.

Chapter 11: Embracing Resilience

As the sun rose the following morning, she was startled to find Jesus leaning over her.

As she saw Jesus bending over her, a surge of emotion overcame her. It was a mix of relief, peace, and overwhelming joy. The sight of his compassionate gaze and the touch of his hand filled her with a sense of serenity and comfort she had never experienced before. The worries and troubles that burdened her heart at that moment seemed to fade away, replaced by a profound sense of love and understanding. Stretching out her hand, she brushed her fingers against his face. His warm smile reassured her as he tenderly kissed her forehead. Gently, he reached out and touched her cheeks, sensing the tears, and asked, "What troubles you, my child?" She gently rested her head against his shoulder and whispered, "Nothing. I am so happy you are here with me." As tears welled up in her eyes, she wept softly, finding solace not only in the presence of Jesus but also in the bittersweet memories that had flooded back to her – memories of the lonely times she had endured.

The resurrection of her abusive childhood memories stirred a turbulent mix of emotions within her. She felt a profound sense of anguish and Fear as the traumatic experiences flooded back, bringing back the pain and suffering she had endured. The memories cast a dark shadow, evoking feelings of vulnerability and distress, and she struggled to cope with the overwhelming surge of emotions that accompanied the recollection of those painful moments. She strode on with determination, her mind resisting the pull of childhood memories. Frustration boiled within her as she lashed at a small stone in her path. She pondered what benefit was there in revisiting the murky waters of her past. Only shadows greeted her, no flicker of pleasant memories to be found. Once again, she found herself consumed by the suffocating embrace of darkness. It was almost unbelievable to her that, after enduring a long and traumatic childhood, she had returned to the very same place she had fought so hard to escape. As she stood there, she felt the presence of Jesus enveloping her. The evening was serene, with the only sounds being the gentle murmur of the sea in the distance and the rhythmic splatter of raindrops falling steadily around her. She leaned against the rough surface of a boulder and gently closed her heavy, exhausted eyes. The sound of the rain subsided, bringing a moment of calm and relief as she drifted into a peaceful slumber. She knew that Jesus was there. As she awoke, the scene before her was simply breathtaking. The many flowers around her displayed myriad colours, glistening with the morning dew. The branches of the trees were adorned with a mist of green leaves, swaying gently in the morning breeze against a sky tinted with the soft hues of roses. Everything - the flowers, the trees, and the earth itself - seemed to be bathed in a majestic light, creating an enchanting and serene atmosphere. She felt an overwhelming sense of peace and tranquillity wash over her as she beheld the stunning scenery. The beauty and serenity of the natural world seemed to fill her with a deep sense of awe and gratitude. It was as if the sheer magnificence of the scene before her had momentarily lifted any worries or burdens from her shoulders, leaving her feeling truly uplifted and connected to the world around her. Immersed in the gentle embrace of the light, she felt the weight of her body, mind, and spirit lift away. In these fleeting moments, the overwhelming tide of pain dissolved; she basked in the all-encompassing glory of Jesus. As she gently closed her eyes, a rush of memories from her childhood cascaded through her mind like a mighty flood. She hesitated to open her eyes again, afraid that someone might be able to peek into her thoughts and perceive the depth of emotions she was reliving. She must have felt vulnerable and exposed when she believed people could read her mind. The idea of having her innermost thoughts and feelings laid bare for others to see would likely have left her feeling anxious, powerless, and invaded. It's frightening and disconcerting to think there's nowhere to hide and no privacy for one's inner world. Despite the chaos and uncertainty, she found solace in the soft, reassuring voice that whispered, "I am here." It was unmistakably the voice of Jesus. She clung to His presence for countless years as her sole source of hope. The young girl's encounter with Jesus in the story brought a profound sense of love and comfort into her life. Jesus was depicted as a source of unwavering strength and compassion, giving her the courage to overcome the trauma of her past experiences. His love was often described as gentle and overwhelming, filling her with a sense of peace and security that contrasted starkly with the turmoil caused by her earthly father's actions.

After discovering a deep faith in Jesus, the young girl experienced a profound sense of comfort and a renewed purpose. His love became a guiding beacon, leading her towards healing and tranquillity. This portrayal of Jesus emphasized his role as a source of unwavering love and support, providing hope and a haven during the girl's challenging times.

In the unfolding story, Jesus's character gradually emerges as a beacon of hope, radiating unwavering compassion and understanding. His profound influence on the young girl becomes a guiding light, offering her solace and support as she navigates the complexities of her emotional turmoil. His presence represents a profound force for change, empowering her with the courage and resilience to confront and overcome the numerous challenges she faces. Ultimately, this leads her to find peace and healing amid the stormy sea of her past experiences. Jesus stood with calm and compassion, his head bowed in reverence. "Just kneel in front of me," he whispered gently. Overwhelmed with emotion, she sank to her knees, feeling a rush of devotion and love for Jesus. "Oh Jesus, I do love you. I am weary of grappling with these overwhelming emotions that have surfaced recently," she confessed, her voice filled with vulnerability and hope. As she poured out her heart, an indescribable feeling of weightlessness and peace enveloped her, as if she was being uplifted and drawn towards the heavens, leaving her with a profound sense of spiritual connection and tranquillity. Her feelings at that moment were a mix of awe and trepidation. As she felt lifted towards heaven, she experienced a profound weightlessness and spiritual elevation. It was as if all the fear, vulnerability, and turmoil that had plagued her had been momentarily lifted away. At that moment, she felt a surge of hope and reassurance, as if a loving presence was cradling her. The awe-inspiring sensation of ascending towards heaven filled her with a serene peace, and for the first time in a long while, she found herself enveloped in a comforting light that seemed to banish the shadows of her past. On that significant day in her adult life, she experienced the beginning of a healing journey that would span many years. A profound sensation gripped her heart as she paused to see herself as a person rather than merely an object.

Realising she was a person and not an object was a profound and pivotal moment for her. It marked the beginning of her journey towards reclaiming her agency and independence. The realization brought a sense of empowerment and liberation, dispelling the long-held notion of being an object subjected to others' actions. It ignited a spark of self-worth and individuality, allowing her to embrace her identity and begin the process of healing from the traumas of her past. With this newfound understanding, she felt a glimmer of hope for a future where she could define herself on her terms and shape her destiny. Initially, she was uncertain about the events unfolding around her. However, she was steadfast in her belief that she was meant to follow Jesus, as she trusted that he would always be there for her. She was acutely aware, deep in her heart, that the path unfolding before her would be fraught with daunting challenges. She knew she must muster all her strength to overcome numerous obstacles and make difficult decisions. And so, with a sense of trepidation and determination, her story carried on.

Chapter 12: A New Horizon

Continuing her story as an adult, she stands at the water's edge, her gaze fixed on the tranquil expanse before her. The ripples on the water's surface echo her journey, from the tumultuous storms of her past to the newfound sense of calm that now envelops her.

As she reflects on the trials and triumphs that have shaped her, a profound sense of gratitude wells up within her. Each undulating wave reminds her of the resilience she has unearthed within herself, propelling her to this new chapter.

With a resolute spirit, she embraces the promise of fresh beginnings, guided by the wisdom and understanding she has gained from her experiences. This horizon, once daunting and unknown, now beckons with the gentle whispers of hope and the enduring strength that has carried her through. Her head was bowed, and her straight, brown hair cascaded over her pale face. The tranquil morning had arrived, casting a serene atmosphere over the landscape. She could finally discern the hills beyond the peaceful water in the distance as she gazed. That morning, she was roused from sleep by the melodic symphony of the birds. Lying on the ground, she savoured the serenade while observing the ever-changing sky overhead. The morning sky was a breathtaking spectacle, painted with intricate strokes of vibrant colours. As the sun began ascent, it cast a warm, golden glow that gently enveloped the horizon. The hues of orange and pink melded seamlessly with the rich, dark blue canvas of the sky. Wisps of fluffy white clouds drifted lazily, catching the first light of dawn and taking on a delicate, rosy hue.

The tranquil expanse of the sky mirrors the calm waters below, creating a harmonious connection between earth and sky. The sunlight danced across the horizon, illuminating the world with a soft, ethereal radiance that whispered promises of a new day. The scene was nothing short of a masterpiece, evoking a sense of serenity and hope as nature unveiled the beauty of a fresh morning. The melodious symphony of the morning birdsong filled her with a profound sense of peace and tranquillity. As the gentle notes of the birds' song floated through the air, they seemed to weave a soothing tapestry around her, momentarily lifting the weight of her burdens. Each trill and chirp was a testament to the resilience of nature, a reminder that beauty and hope still thrived amidst the darkness.

Listening to the birds' song, she felt a glimmer of comfort and reassurance, as if the delicate melodies were whispering messages of encouragement directly to her soul. It was as though the birds were offering companionship, their songs becoming a source of solace in the quiet morning air. In those fleeting moments, the weight of her fears seemed to lift momentarily, and she embraced the simple yet profound beauty of the natural world around her.

As the years passed, she bravely faced the storms. Whenever the wind howled or the rain poured down, terror would grip her nerves, and she would feel a coldness, as if a bucket of icy water had been emptied over her. I can only imagine the immense challenge that must have weighed on her. Despite moments of fleeting safety, her frayed nerves left her grappling with overwhelming shame over her perceived irrational and childish fears. Yet, she exhibited an unwavering resolve to confront and overcome her inner turmoil fiercely. She frequently found herself slipping back into the terrifying realm of her nightmares. Once again, she was the frightened little girl lost in an overwhelming sea of darkness. When her nightmares resurfaced, she was overwhelmed with the same intense fear and vulnerability that she experienced as a frightened little girl. The recurring terror from her past made her feel like she was trapped in a relentless cycle of unease, unable to shake off the paralyzing sense of helplessness. It was a harrowing experience that took a significant toll on her emotional well-being. In the quiet stillness of the night, she found herself alone once more in the small boat. The darkness enveloped her, and her voice echoed into the emptiness. Paralyzed with fear, she struggled to move her hands and feet, only to awaken in a state of panic and distress. These unsettling nightmares haunted her for years; The experience left a lasting impression on her soul. She grew to detest storms and darkness because the nightmares she experienced were hauntingly vivid, leaving her grappling with a terror that seemed more tangible than anything she could ever have imagined.

As she gradually emerged from the clutch of one of her chilling nightmares, her bleary eyes fought to adapt to the dazzling glare. As she jolted awake, her heart pounded in her chest, and her entire body was drenched in sweat, leaving her feeling wholly disoriented and profoundly shaken by the intense grip of her nightmare. The moon cast silver reflections from the crests of the waves while a haunting reddish-brown hue slowly emerged from the sea, adding an eerie and surreal atmosphere to the scene. Her unwavering determination fuelled her relentless pursuit of freedom, serving as a powerful testament to her unyielding resolve in the eyes of everyone around her. Jesus assured her he would never be beyond her reach or call for help, even when she couldn't see him. "I shall be present with you at all times, even though I will be invisible, and you have my faithful promise that this journey you are now on will be a means of developing your inner self. When the flower of love is ready to bloom in your heart, you will be loved in return." The flower of love is often symbolized by the red rose, a timeless representation of love and passion. With its velvety petals and captivating fragrance, the red rose is cherished as a classic romantic symbol, signifying deep affection and desire. The flower's vibrant colour exudes warmth and ardour, evoking strong emotions of love and devotion.

Additionally, the delicate beauty of the red rose encapsulates the tender and enchanting nature of love, making it a cherished emblem of affection in various cultures worldwide. The flower of love, exemplified by the red rose, embodies the essence of romance, expressing love, admiration, and tenderness. As these words were spoken, her tears welled up in her eyes. She crouched at Jesus's feet, sobbing as if her heart would break. She looked up into Jesus's face through the blanket of tears. " I really love you. Oh, forgive me, I can't help my tears," she said. He responded in his usual, gentle voice, "I love you too." without warning, he disappeared. When Jesus suddenly disappeared, she felt a wave of confusion and sadness overwhelming her. It was as if her source of comfort and understanding had vanished instantly, leaving her feeling lost and abandoned. Her heart sank as she tried to comprehend the abrupt absence of the one who had brought her peace and reassurance.

Chapter 13: Finding Hope and Healing

Growing from a little girl into an adult, the journey of finding hope and healing embodies her unwavering resilience and inner strength. Despite the myriad challenges and obstacles encountered along the way, the path toward hope and healing unveils the unyielding power of the human spirit. It is a profoundly personal journey characterized by self-discovery, fortitude, and an unwavering determination to surmount adversity. Embracing the journey of healing presents the opportunity to reclaim her story and sculpt a brighter, more promising future for herself.

Amidst her pain and brokenness, she endured a relentless storm that had battered her since she was a young girl. Jesus saw it all. Not a single raindrop fell, and a sudden gust of wind passed; he was unaware of their presence. Despite this, he understood every heartache she endured. His love for her was immense, evident in how he gazed at her with grace, empathy, and compassion.

Meanwhile, the lurking presence of the devil threatened to unleash storms and destroy her. When you encounter challenges the devil sends, just hold on to Jesus in the boat. As long as Jesus is in the boat, it will not sink." The storms show us that Jesus has full authority and power over everything, including the raging seas, mighty waves, and the devil. He is the Master, lord of the storms, and king of the flood. We can pass through every storm with Him, as the little girl discovered when she grew up into adulthood. Jesus' desire is not to destroy us in the storms but to develop a deeper faith and fruitfulness for his glory. With all of this to hold on to, She found herself in a peaceful spot by the tranquil water's edge, where the gentle waves lapping filled her with a sense of serene tranquillity she sat at the water's edge with the waves gently lapping against the shore; she felt a profound sense of peace and tranquillity enveloping her. The rhythmic sound of the waves was like a soothing lullaby, and the gentle caress of the water against the sand filled her with a sense of serenity. It was as if nature embraced her with its calming presence, washing away her worries and fears with each gentle wave. She found solace in the sea's ebb and flow at that moment, a brief respite from the tumultuous storm within her. She quickly shifted her gaze towards a small boat tethered to a rock. In that instant, she hesitated, as the sight of a boat signified lurking danger to her. She quickly made her way to the boat. No one else was around, so she decided to clamber into it. The afternoon was warm, and she was in the boat, facing the sun. The sun's rays enveloped her in a comforting embrace, painting the sky with a captivating blend of orange and pink that illuminated the vast expanse of the ocean. The sun's warmth created a tranquil haven as she lay in the boat. With her eyes closed, she could feel the sun's radiant touch on her skin, offering a fleeting moment of peace amidst the churning waves. The sun's gentle caress provided a brief respite, casting a soft glow over the boat as if to remind her that, even amid turmoil, there was still light and warmth to be found. She must have drifted off briefly before she awoke, the late afternoon sunlight casting a warm glow around her. She gazed upward and noticed Jesus seated beside her. "Did you have a restful sleep?" he inquired. "I simply dozed off," she admitted. "The sea has a way of lulling you to sleep."

Jesus suggested, "Why don't we take a short sail?" Nervously, she hesitated, her mind flashing back to past unsettling experiences at sea before. "It will be fine," he asserted. "There is not a ripple, not a wave. Trust me." With mounting apprehension, she clutched the side of the boat. Initially, the boat maintained a steady course, inducing a sense of calm as she relied on the presence of Jesus. However, a sudden shudder caused her to panic as the boat appeared on the verge of tipping over. Her grip on the side tightened, and a touch of fear enveloped her.

Jesus leaned in close, his eyes locking with hers, and a soft smile played on his lips as he said, "Isn't this moment just so wonderful?" Despite the warmth in his voice, she couldn't shake the persistent feeling of dread that seemed to linger at the edge of her consciousness, like a gathering storm on the horizon. With every ounce of her being, she willed herself to shake off these unnerving premonitions, but they clung to her like a heavy shroud, casting a shadow over the enchanting encounter. The boat gently "perched on" small, rushing wavelets, causing the bow to push a delicate curtain of fine spray. A faint shiver ran through her as she pondered how long she could endure the journey. Suddenly, the boat changed direction, and instantly, the motion felt smoother. The waves, once rushing at the boat, now seemed to be moving harmoniously alongside it. She enjoyed the tranquil conditions, with no waves and minimal wind. "Sailing along is an amazing feeling of freedom," Jesus shared. She experienced a remarkable calmness on the water for the first time. The water was incredibly calm, with a smooth surface reflecting the sunlight.

Facing the tumultuous storms of her childhood marked just the start of her journey. Overcoming her trials was no easy feat, but now she felt a deep sense of presence and support, knowing that Jesus was with her every step. Through this unwavering faith, she had unearthed unparalleled hope and the victorious blessings that only Jesus could bestow. In the quiet stillness of the night, the fabric of her story begins to unravel, revealing the intricate threads of her journey.

Chapter 14: A Glimpse of Hope

As the young girl blossomed into adulthood, she grappled with profound questions. Why did Jesus allow her to endure such turbulent storms? Over time, she realised that the answer lay in her unwavering faith and her deeply personal connection with Jesus, who had always stood faithfully by her side. He stood by her side, shedding tears, consoling, and empowering her to continue. During the periods when her father was sexually and physically abusing her, she often found herself questioning why she felt as though Jesus had abandoned her in her most desperate hour; she cried out, "Jesus, where were you when I needed you the most?" As she gazed upon the scene, it evoked in her mind the image of Jesus in his most desperate moment on the cross, uttering the anguished prayer, "My God, my God, why have you forsaken me?" The intensity of the moment and the depth of emotion echoed throughout her thoughts, leaving a powerful impression of the weight of Jesus's suffering. Her heart ached for understanding as she grappled with inner turmoil. The devil's whispers taunted her, sowing seeds of doubt about the goodness of Jesus; using the little girl's suffering as evidence within her thoughts, she held the unwavering belief that Jesus was inherently good and never turned a blind eye to the sins that inflicted pain upon children. He felt deep sorrow for all sins and detested them. Her solace came from knowing that Jesus could empathize with the pain of abuse. He endured tremendous mistreatment and ultimately sacrificed his life to grant her the life she deserved. Throughout her life, he was a beacon of hope in her present and future. He promised to overcome her painful past despite her hardships and find victory. This hope stayed with her into adulthood, shaping her outlook and guiding her decisions. Even when she felt alone, Jesus saw her suffering and shared her pain. Jesus detests injustice and grieved with her. He did not intend for her to experience the storms she had to endure. As this young woman matured, she found herself confronted by yet another overwhelming challenge – the profound, gut-wrenching pain of losing her own beloved daughter, a storm of grief that threatened to consume her. She was utterly devastated by the loss of her little girl, feeling as if she was trapped in the eye of an unrelenting emotional storm. Overwhelmed by grief, she experienced an unyielding torrent of emotions, from profound sadness and despair to profound loss, as if the weight of her loss bore down on her with unrelenting force. Each day felt like navigating through a storm, with waves of anguish and heartache crashing over her, leaving her feeling shattered and adrift in an unforgiving sea of sorrow. The oppressive darkness descended upon her, wrapping around her like a suffocating shroud, threatening to engulf her entirely. Her daughter's radiant smile lit up the room with warmth and joy. She possessed a loving character, always quick to show kindness and compassion to those around her. Her empathy and nurturing nature endeared her to everyone she met. She was in disbelief as the reality sunk in - her own daughter was no longer with her. She felt utterly powerless, knowing that her daughter had been fighting her own battles, and she couldn't help. She longed to wake up from what felt like a never-ending nightmare, hoping that her daughter would still be by her side. However, as she finally awoke, the harsh truth hit her like a ton of bricks - it was all too real. She was overwhelmed with unbearable pain. It felt as if her heart had been ripped out, and she was viewing life through a grey cloud, living in a shadow. She could only express her anguish through misty eyes, desperately asking, "Where is my little girl?" There were many beautiful things for her right here in this place. She longed to hold her close, to guide her through the world and all its wonders. She could only picture her daughter's beaming smile as a vibrant autumn leaf descended from above. Why was she suddenly caught amid this relentless storm? How could Jesus, the all-loving person she had trusted and who had previously guided her safely, now seem to be leading her deeper into this unforgiving storm? At that moment, she felt like the little girl on the boat again. Fear gripped her tightly. Once again, she couldn't help but wonder why Jesus was not there with her. Her desperation was overwhelming. The storm unleashed its fury, descending from the lofty peaks of the surrounding mountains and cliffs. This time, the storm was exceptionally fierce, with the high winds violently churning the sea into towering, menacing waves. She had never before encountered such a terrifying and overwhelming storm. Once more, she found herself in the same helpless state, like the frightened little girl she had once been, desperately straining at the oars. The question echoed in her mind: Where was Jesus? The mast of the boat thrashed violently as the vessel rocked in every direction. On that day, her personal faith was severely shaken, leaving her unable to perceive or connect with Jesus. The powerful storm raged with relentless fury, unleashing torrents of rain and howling winds. Amidst the heaving tempest, she was struck by the devastating loss of her own daughter, a heart-wrenching tragedy amidst the chaos of the storm. The unrelenting storm stretched endlessly, providing no respite or way out. The intense emotions that consumed her after losing her daughter were a complex mix of sorrow, despair, and a profound sense of emptiness. How would she find her way back to tranquillity and peace once more? As the storm continued to rage within her, she realised that finding calmness on the water again was not the end of her story but a new chapter in her life where her journey would continue.